THE **CURSE** OF HANNAH

CJ KNAPP

CHAPTER 1

The morning is hot and crazy. There are no rules here. Hannah had her "miserable" face on. The young girl twisted her head to look at the New Jersey clothes in the obscene walk-in closet where all her navy blue clothes were tucked away. She rolled over to her little flat belly, jutted her pointy elbows into the mushy mattress and held her head up on cupped hands. She felt the collar on her nightie whispering against her neck from that ridiculous ceiling fan. A soft knock on her bedroom door. *Tap, tap, tap.*

A muffled voice entreated, "Hannah. Hannah, get up. Time for breakfast. Almadine's making waffles *and* fried chicken."

The little girl in bed mimed barfing on her pillow, poking her index finger into her pink rounded mouth and pumping. Her lips curled into a cool and haughty smile as she answered, "Minutam."

Arriona on the other side of the door frowned. She knew when she was being patronized. She rapped on the door once more and said louder and sharper, "Breakfast." Then she spun on one foot and headed down the long staircase to the kitchen where Gramma Sophie was already seated, wearing her favorite terrycloth robe and sipping her morning coffee.

Sophie's blonde curls were pinned up on the top of her head, but a few ringlets had escaped and lay close to her cheeks and neck. Angus Clark noticed these golden strands and reached over and lifted one that threatened her vision. Sophie caught his hand and pressed it to her lips.

"I've got to get going Mr. and Mrs. Clark."

"Oh Laura, you're such a tease."

Laura enjoyed seeing her mom and Angus so in love. Who would've ever thought her mother would marry again after Harry; Laura and Mandy Rose's now deceased father.

Arriona sat at the table and Almadine plunked down a steaming plate of waffles and fried chicken. "Do we have syrup, Almadine?"

"Of course chile, here tis all warmed up special for you."

Arriona's chest swelled, and she chirped, "Thank you, thank you."

Hannah descended the stairs and stood watching all this; her face still except for a twisted upper lip as though none of this interested her. *La belle indifference.*

Sophie smiled at her granddaughter and called in a sugary voice, "Honey, come sit down. Are you hungry?"

"I want some grapefruit juice and a piece of dry toast."

Almadine dragged a chair out and said, "Sit right here. No grapefruit juice, just orange juice and buttered toast coming right up." Almadine refused to be bullied by the sullen girl.

Hannah sashayed to the table and repositioned the proffered chair closer to where Laura sat, distancing herself from Arriona, who was busy drowning her breakfast in more maple syrup while she chewed on a piece of chicken breast.

Sophie's eyes brimmed as she peered at Hannah. She was concerned. It had been almost three months since the girl came home. Everyone kept advising her to be patient. Kept saying, "She'll come around in time." Sophie's curls swayed as she shook her head. The child was unhappy. Nothing helped. Her schoolwork was excellent. However, her teachers said, "She doesn't mix well with the other children. When she agrees to have anything to do with them, she becomes peeved if she can't be in command." She didn't strike out physically. Well, except for that one time she raked her fingernails down the face of the boy sitting behind her in class. They'd had to call it self-defense because he'd pulled her hair first. The poor kid probably had a crush on her. She was strikingly pretty and quiz-kid smart. She'd inherited her father Clyde's green eyes and strawberry curls and her mother's tilted nose, made exotic by the slightly slanted nostrils; complements of Clyde.

The psychological counseling wasn't working. The child was too intelligent not to see what they were attempting to accomplish. Sophie wanted a new counselor, wanted someone to start fresh with Hannah.

"Sophie, Sophie." Angus squeezed her upper arm to get her attention.

"What? Oh Angus, sorry, guess I was off somewhere."

"Do you know if the chauffer has agreed to stay on with us?"

"Yes, I talked him into not leaving. I don't have the full story yet, don't know why he wanted to quit. I gave him a raise in salary."

"Is he taking the girls to school?"

"Yes." Sophie watched Hannah taking dainty bites of her toast as though it would poison her if she ate it as though she liked it. Sophie continued. "Finish up girls, get ready for Cedric to take you to school."

Hannah scraped her chair back and bolted for the stairs. Arriona wiped her chin and turned her knees sideways to get up and go back upstairs to dress for school.

"Don't worry, Mama. Things will get better." Laura kissed her mother's cheek and turned to leave.

Sophie sighed. "Yeah, but when?"

With both of the girl upstairs getting ready for school, Angus felt free to speak. "We have a new undercover detective starting tomorrow. A woman. She came to us from another precinct. Lots of experience finding people who don't want to be found.

Sophie's eyes filled with water. "Yeah, like Mandy Rose…" Her voice trailed off. "Don't want to be found."

Less than an hour later, the house was quiet. Sophie sat staring at her cold cup of coffee, the cream on top separated and casting a blue shadow. "Where's my daughter? Where's my Mandy?"

No answer came from the swirling air of the huge ceiling fan, though Sophie stared up at it.

CHAPTER 2

Clyde Boudreaux made an early exit from the Bokum mansion, opting to skip breakfast and early morning conversation. Mandy Rose's abandoned Thunderbird was now his. He thrust his hand into his breast pocket and fingered the tiny silk pouch that held a curly tendril of her chestnut hair.

He loved the feeling of driving this machine. On the road in no time, the air conditioning cooled his face as he sped along the highway. *Where is she?* She had his gris-gris. His personal totem. His grandfather's gift to him. Its great powers still not fully explored. He believed this totally. Even more amazing, Mandy believed in it. She'd watched it perform miracles. She couldn't deny its role in busting him out of that mental asylum.

He pulled into a shop that featured a huge coffee cup as an invitation; feeling a pang of guilt as he slammed the door to the T-Bird. How quickly he'd become used to not being poor. The place was cool and breezy with overhead fans adding to the ambiance. He took a table that was meant for four as he wanted room.

Spreading his notes on the table top was soothing as he ran his fingertips over the shiny maple wood. The names on the lists kept growing. Today would be busy. He'd be showing Mandy Rose's photo, asking the same question. "Have you seen this woman?"

"Sir, sir."

Clyde gave a little jerk of his head as he looked up into eyes as green as his own and skin the color of milky cocoa.

"Do you need a menu, or do you know what you want?" There was just the tiniest hint of irritation.

He found his tongue. "I know. Bring me some sausages and scrambled eggs with rye toast and coffee."

Another question. "Buttered?"

"Yes, please."

"I'll bring you some peach jam too." It wasn't a question. The waitress shifted her rounded hip and smiled at her handsome customer. Clyde grinned back and covered the exposed papers with both hands. She touched his smooth forearm, marveling at the lack of hair or fat; all muscle.

He watched her walk away, felt a pleasant urge. No desire to complicate his life right now, he chose to ignore his awakened lust. He had his daughter to think of and her mother to find. But he wasn't dead yet, was he? No surprise when later along with the bill was a scrap of paper, scrawled with the message: "Mimi, call me" and a telephone number he recognized as New Orleans.

Clyde brought the bill to the cash register where a beetle-browed man with plastered-down, gray hair took his money. Mimi was busy with a crowded table; two overweight women who wore pink bandanas and half a dozen kids; one of whom was bopping another on the head with her menu.

The scrap of paper went into his back pocket where it might remain or not.

Back in Mandy's car, the leather seats were already hot and working on sticky. He jacked up the AC and continued on his mission to find Mandy, but his attention was divided. "Hmmm, Mimi. Was that her real name or a pet name?" Her ring finger was naked.

He thought, So is mine.

<h1 style="text-align:center">CHAPTER 3</h1>

Clyde fingered the photo of Mandy Rose. It was a good likeness. He knew he'd wear out some shoe leather showing it around in the French Quarter. He wanted Hannah to know her mother. A worthy objective, but where was Mandy? Who had she fallen in with? What doors had been opened for her with his gris-gris? It was a powerful amulet in the hands of the uninitiated. She could be in danger. She could now be a mere shadow of the Mandy Rose he knew as his lover and the mother of their daughter.

The afternoon had slipped away and the city was turning dark early under cloudy skies.

Clyde pulled the T-Bird into what appeared to be a safe place for such an expensive vehicle. The apartment building had visitor parking, and he could see past a wrought iron enclosure to a patio area with a large swimming pool. High-pitched voices of children reached his ears, and he clapped his hands over them. Pain bubbled up from his chest thinking of Hannah. He pocketed the ignition keys, left on foot and headed into the seedier portions of New Orleans.

"Cabby, take me to LaRue."

The cab driver twisted in his seat to get a better look at Clyde.

"Oh no, Mistah. I don't think you wants to go there."

Clyde tried not to breathe in the stale smoke and rancid spices stinking up the taxi's interior but answered in the affirmative. "Yes, yes, I do, and I'm gonna want you to wait for me in the street when I go into a few different place."

"Nope, nope, nope, I ain't got no death wish. Haul right outta my cab. I mean now."

Clyde lifted his butt from the seat and pulled out a wad of twenties, held it in front of the driver's nose then shoved it in a lump under the brown tattered cap the cabbie wore. The bills caught an errant slice of sunlight making a tasty green statement of wealth, and the man reached up with brown gnarled fingers to touch the roll of bills. Clyde yanked it back, said, "Okay, if you're chicken shit, I'll get a ride from someone else."

With the huge wad retrieved, Clyde, pulled his arm back and made to open the door to leave.

"No suh, no suh, you jest wait a minute. I'll take yah if you're good for your word."

Clyde peeled off one twenty and chucked it onto the front passenger seat where it floated down out of sight. It was snatched. It disappeared into a paisley green and purple shirt pocket. "So, we have a deal?"

"Yes suh, yes suh, a deal."

The cab's engine made an odd rumbling sound but pulled out without ceremony. Night was turning a rich shade of purple and shadows were deepening. Within five minutes, they were in narrower streets with fewer lights. Many poles hung empty.

Clyde shouted, "Stop, I'm going in here."

The cabby stared at Clyde with rounded eyes that almost smelled of fear.

Clyde held up the wad of money again and said, "Keep your motor idling. Leave if you want to."

The driver leaned toward the steering wheel and sank down into his seat until little of him was visible.

Clyde arched his back and felt his pocket for his ivory handled switchblade and patted his lower back where his Beretta nestled in his waistband holster. He cleared his throat.

He left the cab on the curb looking empty and mysterious. Clyde squared his shoulders and headed toward a weathered red door that was older than his grandfather would've been if he were still alive and had not been lynched. High up on the door was a two by four-inch rectangular window with bullet glass in it. It was dirty yellow from an unknown source of light coming from inside the building. Clyde rose up and tilted his head back to peer into the urine-yellow slit. A shadow flitted across it.

Clyde heard himself swallow noisily, tapped his Beretta once more, and using the side of his fist, thumped three times on the door. The slow idle of a vehicle revved into the roar of acceleration. The sound came from behind him. He twisted his head, hoping he was wrong. He caught two red taillights growing rapidly smaller as they disappeared up the dark street. He swore, "Fucking cabby."

The creaking sound of old wood and unoiled hinges broke his irritated mood, replacing it with a familiar enemy; fear. His old companion; fear of the unknown. His heart drummed. His forehead beaded with dollops of sweat.

"Yah, whaddya want?"

Clyde looked up at a huge blond guy dressed all in black with a shoulder holster in full view. Clyde's voice cracked a bit as he tried to recoup his cool. "Sorry to disturb. I'm looking for a girl. Was hoping you could help."

"Why should I? We're busy, not open to the public and that's you. Now take a hike."

Clyde held up the shiny photo of Mandy Rose. "This is her."

The man took a quick look and jerked his head back. "Get out of here before you wish you did." The huge man backed away without turning and slammed the ancient door.

Clyde stood there with the moon for company and rocked back on his heels. He headed up the street, welcoming the sight of more people and more lights. After walking a mile or more, cursing the cabby a few more times, he headed into a bar with a red and yellow neon sign that read "Bubba's Clams." Yeah, that's what he wanted. Beer and clams. He was hungry and feeling a bit down. The succulent smells made his mouth water.

There was an empty stool at the bar. He headed for it. The place was chock full of good old boys. Fine with him. After he ordered, he took the picture of Mandy Rose out and studied it as he waited for his food.

A slender hand reached over and tapped the photo. "Is that your wife?"

Clyde turned to see a naked shoulder just below a pretty face. A familiar face. His jaw dropped. "Mimi."

CHAPTER 4

Mandy Rose Bokum preferred her new name. She wet her finger and traced it in the layer of dust on top of the old sideboard in her room; the only piece of furniture except for the army cot she slept on, sat on and ate on. She used cursive to spell out Bianca. She needed no last name. She wrote Bianca on her forehead again in cursive.

Scratching her head, feeling the bristles of hair grown in from her homemade shearing reminded her of what her appearance was now. She was clothed in a shapeless gown of muslin, no descriptive color. It reached almost to her heels. Her feet still wore the expensive black flats she'd worn when she left home; that obscene mansion. Was Hannah living there now? At least Harry wasn't. He was dead. She could still feel and smell his fetid breath as he lay on top of her, his forelock of dark hair brushing her little baby face as he spoke huskily. "Don't move little girl. Let Daddy finish."

Would this memory never fade? Mandy, now Bianca, shook her head to loosen that hideous recall. She spoke out loud to the four walls. "Burn in Hell."

Mandy was learning some ancient revenge spells. If Harry was still among the living, one of these fine curses would fix that. Make him suffer.

She sat down on the cot and tucked her legs deep underneath her baggy gown and chanted. Her legs folded easily next to her bottom as her stomach wasn't felt, so sunken was it from the pounds shed.

She wanted to kill Mama Luna. Power hungry priestess. That bitch was behind the taking of Clyde's gris-gris. The woman had seen it glimmering and shining right through Mandy's pocket. Her shorn head had not protected her. Mandy craved revenge. She knew some of the gris-gris's power would remain with her, just as it would with Clyde. The depth of her fury would feed the malevolent energy that lived in her breast. Mama Luna would have to pay.

9

That gris-gris was powerful, a driving force Mandy could never comprehend. For that matter, neither could Clyde.

CHAPTER 5

Laura said to Cassy, "What do you think, Cass? Where the hell is my sister?"

Cassy tilted her head back as though the answer might be on the ceiling. "Mandy Rose has always been a mystery to me. I can't imagine being molested by your own father and not telling anyone. So, I can't gauge how deeply that affected her. I never knew my father. He was basically a sperm donor, like a lot of Black men back then. I've always thought a big part of that was society. Those men couldn't get a break. They couldn't earn a decent living to support a family. They were finished before they got started, so they gave up. History has a way of repeating itself." Cassy's eyes brimmed, becoming chocolate-pools of sadness. "Arriona's daddy was no exception. He was a kind man, just not very strong." Cassy's head drooped, then she raised her eyes to Laura's. "And that's not what you asked me about, is it?" She continued. "When Mandy left she did so in a weird way. I remember she cut all her hair off and stole Clyde's magic Voodoo charm."

"I know." Pause. "Clyde thinks she's somewhere in New Orleans. That Voodoo charm; his gris-gris…" another pause, "…could help her or it could attract some very bad people. There're a lot of very bad people in New Orleans."

"I don't know much about Voodoo. Maybe we should help Clyde." Then as an afterthought, she said, "The guy is disturbingly good looking."

"I thought you were gay?"

"I am. Well, maybe not one hundred percent. After all, I am Arriona's mother and that wasn't a virgin birth."

"Christ Cassy, if you're hot for Clyde, you're in for a crap load of trouble."

Cassandra averted her eyes; a sure sign of not wanting to be "made."

The two cops let the subject drop, like the hot potato it was.

Sophie scuffled in, still wearing her battered mules. She held a glass of something that shimmered, that had a slice of lime floating on the top. "What's going on girls?"

"Not a thing, Mama. Not a thing."

<h1 style="text-align:center">CHAPTER 6</h1>

Captain Richard Sloane drummed his fingers on his polished desk while he waited for Detective Angus Clark to show up for the two-person meeting. It was a short wait.

Angus entered the captain's office after a brief knock on the frosted glass door. The captain rearranged a few papers, flattened them, then said, "Sit down Angus."

Angus fell into the seat facing Rick's desk.

"You know we're not staying ahead of these traffickers. What we accomplished was good, but we need to do more."

Angus nodded and ran his hand over the top of his now almost bald head.

Crack, crack, crack. Three sharp knocks on the door made both men stare. Angus twisted in his seat to get a better view of whoever was insisting entry into a private meeting.

Not waiting for permission, Sargent Cassidy charged in.

Captain Sloan reacted, barked, "Trudy, what is it?"

Out of breath, Cassidy puffed out the words, "Girls' taken."

"What? When?"

"Within the hour. Two of them. Sisters."

"From where, Trudy?" Sloane's phone was in his hand and on his ear.

Trudy pressed on her chest as her breathing slowed. "That carnival on Rivoli Street."

Sloane gave the location and the order to send out squad cars.

"What do we know?"

"They were seen getting into a white van. One girl was lifted and put inside and the other, a bit, bigger followed suit. The story goes there was a puppy involved. The guy held the pooch in his arms. The dog went in first, then the girls. The door was slammed shut and locked and the man jumped in the shotgun seat. Before the door even closed, the driver peeled off."

"Were these kids there alone?"

"The girls' mother was getting hot dogs. When she got back to where she left them, they were gone."

"Witnesses?"

"Two late teen boys who'd been watching the girls. Also, an elderly lady nearby, seated on a resting bench. Apparently she'd been admiring the puppy. According to the young boys, she went scurrying off. She disappeared into the crowd. All they could say about her was that she was real old and dressed in black. Not a good wit I'm thinking."

"Do we have a description?"

"Both boys agree, they couldn't see the man's face. He wore a baseball cap pulled down hiding his eyes and putting the rest of his face in shadow."

"Where are these boys?"

"They'll be here soon."

"Angus, we'll have this discussion later. I want you to interview those boys."

"Yes Captain, times already going by."

Detective Angus Clark looked straight at Sargent Trudy Cassidy, his face a mixture of feelings. His furrowed brows matched the pencil line of his mouth and created a white halo around his lips. "Put those boys in room number three."

Angus strode out of the office.

<h1 style="text-align:center">CHAPTER 7</h1>

Angus made a quick stop in the men's room before continuing to interrogation room number three. As he got a bit older he'd learned it was better to use the urinal before going into a situation that might take more time than he thought. He loved that he and Sophie would grow older together. After he washed his hands, he peered into the lavatory mirror and for good measure splashed some cold water on his face; dried it with a brown paper towel.

As he approached the room occupied by the two boys, he could hear them laughing. A somewhat strange sound as their nervousness at being in a police station interrupted their youthful voices with a mixture of bravado and mirth. He regretted he'd never become a father.

He tightened his jaw and slammed into the room. The boyish cajoling stopped. Angus didn't speak right away. He took in the expressions on the youthful faces and registered his first impressions. Always revealing. One boy, though seated, looked to be almost six feet tall. He wore his dirty blond hair long and his startling blue eyes were slitted as he eyeballed the police officer in front of him. He was movie star good-looking. He wore his shirt collar up and had a bulky gold colored watch on his slender wrist, probably a Rolex knockoff. This was the Alpha male.

The other boy had long hair also; medium brown with eyes that were opened wide, like coffee-colored ancient coins. He was chubby. His puffy fingers played with each other on the worn and scarred grayish table. The boy's shirt was a faded purple tee with a stretched-out neck. The image on the front appeared to, once upon a time, say Coors in cursive.

Angus sat opposite the boys and got eye contact with the pudgy one and started in.

"What's your name, son?"

"Uh, Leon."

"Last name too, please." Angus pulled out a five-inch tablet, grabbed the attached pen that swung from it and wrote, "Leon."

"Uh, Leon Shalinski."

"Age?"

"Uh, eighteen last month."

Angus wrote. Without looking up all the way, he said, "And yours, son?"

Immediate retort. "I ain't your son."

"Okay, fine. Just tell me your name, please."

"It's Mike. Mike Liberty. And I'm almost nineteen."

"Thanks. I want you both to tell me exactly what you saw when the girls were taken."

Mike said, "Is there a reward for information leading to an arrest?"

Angus twisted his jaw back and forth, said, "Too early to know anything about rewards. It's possible."

Mike continued as he leaned back. "I'd rather wait until that's the story."

Angus stood up so fast his chair crashed over behind him. He slammed his palms down on the long table. "Those two girls were kidnapped. We can't waste time. Their lives could be in danger."

Mike said, "I want a lawyer."

"Mike, you and Leon are not accused of anything. No reason for lawyering up. Unless you choose to be charged with obstruction of justice."

Leon was now sweating large droplets that gathered on the sides of his wide nose. "Mikey, we need to tell what we saw."

Mike leaned back a bit more and folded his arms over his chest.

Angus tried again. He reached down and picked up his chair, scraped it into place and fell into it with a *thump*. "Leon, please tell me what you saw, just as you remember it."

Leon caste a fast glance at Mike, then seemed to make his own decision. "Officer, we was scoping out those girls, you know watching them, not being obvious. Making like we were cool, not interested. Then this guy walks up to them, and he's got this kind of like beige puppy with floppy ears in his arms. The girls go all gushy over the dog, and he's telling them some kind of story. The guy's walking toward the back of the van and they follow him; like they were gonna help him or something. He puts the dog inside, all the time still talking to the girls."

"Could you hear what he was saying?"

"No, but I could tell it was like real friendly."

"What did he look like Leon?"

Mike piped up. "You're giving away all the facts, stupid."

Angus said, "Shut up."

"Leon, what did this guy look like?"

Leon took a deep breath and looked off to the side as he racked his brain trying to remember. "He was not fat or skinny. Kind of in-between. He was a white dude. He had a baseball cap on, but I could tell he had dark hair, 'cause he had a ponytail that stuck out of the bottom of it."

"What color was the hat?"

"Either black or dark blue."

"Was there an emblem on the hat?"

"Yeah, I think it was like a flag, like yah know, cur flag."

"You mean an American flag?"

"Yep, that's it, an American flag."

"How about his clothes?"

"Jeans, washed out, yah know, like acid-washed jeans. Shirt was also faded blue denim."

"Shoes?"

"Dunnoh, didn't notice them."

"You're doing great, Leon. Anything else?"

"One thing. He had a big ruby ring on his pointer finger."

"Leon, you're amazing. You'd make a good detective."

Leon blushed. The compliment pleased him.

Now Mike wanted in. The boy unfolded his long arms and laid one of them around Leon's shoulders.

Leon's mouth clamped shut.

"Yeah, I remember that red ring too. It had a big square red stone. It looked kind of dangerous; like a one finger brass knuckle." Not wanting to be outdone and maybe left out if there was reward money in the future, Mike went on. "I did hear some stuff. The guy was talking kind of low and turning the puppy so the chicks could see its face, then like it was a newborn baby he put it real gentle-like into the truck. The chicks were making those "awwwww" sounds, like when something is cute or adorable. Kinda gushy sounds. Dudes never make that sound."

Leon pushed Mike's arm away, seemingly emboldened by Angus's acceptance. "Yeah, but I heard a different sound too. After the guy put the puppy into the van and the younger girl crawled in, he pushed the older one in and she made a scared sound."

"What did she say?"

"It came out sharp. She said, 'Hey.' She said more that I couldn't hear 'cause her head was in the van. Then the guy shoved her all the way in; pushed her hard on her butt. Then he slammed the doors shut and twisted the lock on them. Next, he ran around and got in the passenger front seat and even before the door was all the way shut, they peeled off. There was a gravelly rooster tail from the tires."

Angus nodded approvingly. "Did either of you get any of the license plate numbers?"

Leon shook his head.

Mike said, "I looked at it after the guy took off, but it was blurry, like the plate had something covering it, like mud or something."

Angus decided to capitalize on Mike's newfound agreeableness. "Do you agree on the clothes this guy wore?"

"Yeah, all dungarees. Blue and baseball hat. A white guy. I could see his hands better than his face. And yep, a ponytail."

"Did you boys drive here?"

"Yeah, followed a broad cop. A good looker. A redhead."

Angus suppressed a smile as he stood up. "You boys did a good job. You can go now."

Mike had his last say. "Uh, will you let us know if there's a reward?"

Angus rolled his eyes. "Sure, we'll let you know. We may want to talk to you boys again. Leave your names and telephone numbers at the front desk."

Leon found his tongue. "Okay, no problem."

Mike gave an army salute in agreement.

And they were gone.

CHAPTER 8

Mandy Rose had a meeting to go to. No, not a meeting, a ceremony. She was happy to be getting out of her one room. Mama Luna would preside, or so she was told. Mandy went to the tiny sink and turned on both faucets to get a heavier stream of water. No soap of any kind, she cupped her hands, filled them and splashed her face with the cool water. She bowed her head and wet her short scruffy hair. She didn't know what to expect at the gathering. She knew it would last for hours and into the next day. She filled her cupped hands again and dropped one hand under her gown to cleanse between her legs. Next, she plopped more under each arm, got her armpits drenched; without shaving there was more hair there than on her head. Mandy Rose regretted cutting all her hair off; wished she'd left it long, if only to hide behind. The only window in her room had raggedy gray drapes that hung from a rusty curtain rod at an odd angle. These would do to dry herself. Sufficiently dry, she dropped onto the cot and folded her hands around her bent knees to wait.

An hour passed. She didn't dare fall asleep. What if the workers came, and she didn't hear them at the door? What if they left and told the priestess she didn't wait for them? She'd been advised that her acceptance to this ceremony made others jealous. They might lie. Maybe try to take her place. She dozed.

A low murmuring sound made its way into Mandy's consciousness. She bit her tongue to see if she was dreaming, drawing blood. She sat up and leaned toward the locked door. Yes, the voices came from outside her room in the hallway. She didn't move. Her heart thumped and an icy chill draped down around her neck and shoulders. A funereal shawl.

Now the words became clearer. "Who was conceived by the holy spirit, born of the Virgin Mary?"

What was required of her? She heard them begin to pray. Should she join in saying the Apostles' Creed? Should she remain silent? She stalled, unsure of what to do. She sat and waited in a cold sweat.

A rapping began. A gentle *tap, tap, tap*. Mandy Rose pushed herself off the cot and putting one foot after the other, she stood facing the door. The tapping continued, never getting any louder. Light taps in a perfectly balanced cadence.

Tap, tap, tap.

CHAPTER 9

"What's wrong, Sophie? You look dejected."

Sophie put both hands around her cup of coffee as she sat at the breakfast table, then looked straight into Angus's eyes before she answered, "Honey, I'm not sure what worries me the most. Mandy Rose taking off again and we're no closer to finding her. Clyde keeps insisting she's somewhere in New Orleans, but so far, he's not finding her. I'm glad he's living here with us because I think it's good for Hannah." Now Sophie ran her hand across her forehead. "But even more, I'm so upset that Hannah isn't coming around. She's distant and always angry. I can't get through to her. Maybe we need to find a different psychologist."

Angus moved to stand behind Sophie's chair, put both arms around her and kissed the top of her head.

Sophie sighed.

Angus said, "I know this is hard for you, dearest."

"Yes, and everyone else has places to go. Laura and Cassy are busy being cops, and I love that." She paused. "Even Arriona and Hannah have school. Speaking of Arriona, she's not saying much, but the other day, Hannah refused to speak English, instead bombarded her with French. I know it was meant to intimidate."

Angus bent down beside Sophie and put one hand on her lap, balancing on his haunches. "What do you think we should do?"

"I don't know. Clyde has tried to get close to her. She shuts him out too. The only time she warms up is if she sees him talking with Arriona. It's like she won't accept him, but she doesn't want Arriona to have him."

Angus rubbed his thumb on Sophie's thigh. The scruffy material made a soft scratchy sound in the silence.

Mr. and Mrs. Angus Clark were at a loss for answers.

Sophie pushed her coffee cup away and shook her head with new resolve. "I'll call another psychologist for Hannah. Maybe that will help."

Angus stood and said, "Why not have Arriona go also? That might make Hannah feel less like she's the problem in all of this."

Sophie's eyes widened, two blue saucers. She tilted her head. "That might work. I'll try anything."

Laura and Cassy both on the run, entered the kitchen. Laura grabbed her mother's coffee and took a couple of swigs, then offered the almost empty cup to Cassy.

Cassy put her hand up in a stop gesture and yelped. "That's your mother's."

"She doesn't mind."

"Yeah Laura, but I do. It was probably tasting perfect."

Laura gave a guilty chuckle and the dark mood lifted a bit.

Angus said, "You gals can get coffee and maybe doughnuts at the precinct."

"Yeah, yeah, Angus. We know." Laura hugged her mother and planted a big smacker on her cheek. Sophie looked at Cassy and held an arm out.

Cassy read the invitation and gave Sophie a one-armed embrace.

Angus hugged Sophie again. He and the girls all left for headquarters. They had work to do. Kidnappers to catch. Traffickers to bring in and put where they belonged.

Soon the only sound was the steady hum of the huge silver refrigerator and the background buzzing of the massive air-condition unit.

Sophie used her spoon to ladle up the tiny remains of the cold coffee at the bottom of her cup and smiled at the thought of Laura stealing a few sips.

Chapter 10

Mandy Rose used both hands to smooth down her thin gown. She reached for the twine that held her sandals in place and tucked the dangling ends under her naked heels. She stood as still as a listening mouse. The praying stopped. The tapping quietened. A soft raspy intonation of her new name followed.

"Bee yan kah… Bee yan kah."

Second thoughts attacked her. She pressed a closed fist to her heart. She must open the door.

"Bee yan kah."

She unfastened the lock, slid it to the left and closed her hand around the copper doorknob, twisted and pulled.

Two acolytes stood there, garbed in long robes, white as summer clouds. Titanium white stripes crawled down both cheeks in stark comparison to their inky blue-black skin. What mimicked white railroad tracks spanned each of their foreheads, completing the picture. They were beautiful. About five foot three or four and slight of build. Mandy guessed their gender as female.

One spoke. "Are you ready, Bianca?"

Mandy was more thrilled than scared. Her body pulsated with a strange brand of eroticism. An overpowering sensation of desire. She pressed her hand tightly to her pubic area and experienced a new awakening never before encountered. Her voice echoed strangely to her own ears. "I'm ready."

Each of the visitors linked their bare black arms through her snowy white elbows as they led her away. She hesitated, said, "I should close the door."

"No need, you won't ever be back here."

Mandy didn't respond, somehow knew that's how it was meant to be.

They stayed linked together and made their way into the street that had turned into a purple hazy darkness, tinged with fear and promise. Others from blackened door stoops watched the small procession as it headed toward a suspected Voodoo habitat. Eyes glistened from reflected moonlight with partial knowledge of what might be going to happen to the girl between the two initiates. The onlookers were torn between horror and envy.

The trio didn't have far to walk. Mandy Rose concluded that her room had been used before. Her mind began a freakish dance, racing between thrilling anticipation to a roller coaster dive with no visible bottom.

Steered into a sidewalk stairwell with black wrought iron rails, they submerged into a basement apartment. Her captors squeezed her in-between them and managed to go to the bottom of the stairs as one unit. She wondered if they would tackle her if she broke free and made a run for it. A dark brown door opened as they arrived.

A giant of a man took her shoulders; pulled her inside. He too wore a white outfit, drawstring pants instead of a gown. His face was also black and shiny with sweat. There was one horizontal stripe under each magnificent chocolate brown eye. The two women waited while this monster of a man led Mandy into a huge room. If it was ever part of a living arrangement, all the walls had been torn down.

The gleaming altar had about twenty totems on display. Sitting on the floor on either side were people, also in long white gowns. Most had dark skin, but not all. There was a life-size statue of the Virgin Mary, likely made of plaster. Her robe was Robin's egg blue; her face pale with pink cheeks. A beatific smile on closed rosebud lips. Pinned to a corkboard were numerous neutral colored rag dolls, Voodoo dolls, some with faces, most blank, devoid of features. All the light in the room came from candles. Tall white candles, casting eerie flickering shadows.

Everyone in the room was staring at her.

Her mouth fell open when she spotted a live goat tied to a pillar almost behind the display of totems. The shock that grabbed her, shook her and made her breath push out a squeaky whoosh was the small glass case that was somehow adhered to the wall. It held her gris-gris. No, Clyde's gris-gris. Then a bolt of metanoia. No, Clyde's grandfather's gris-gris. The man who was lynched with his shoes on. The man who gave Clyde, his beloved grandson, this very same gris-gris. One possessed of untold power. Unmatched power. No wonder it was stolen. Did its power make her come here to New Orleans? Had it overridden her own will?

The man pushed down on her shoulders, forcing her to kneel in front of the display. The altar.

The chanting began.

It was an odd mixture of Catholic prayers and words Mandy Rose remembered hearing Clyde use. Worshipping ancestors, she knew was an important part of the Voodoo religion. She knew what was going on. They were trying to contact Clyde's grandfather. They recognized the gris-gris.

Her heart hammered against her ribs. *Ba boom, ba boom, ba boom. Oh* my God. *Do these people still do human sacrifices? Is this my last day on Earth? Will I die here tonight? No one will ever know what happened to me.* She looked up at the suspended gris-gris. Not knowing what else to do, she made the sign of the cross, clasped her hands and held them to her chest.

The chanting rose in volume. Then fell off only to rise again in a crescendo so bold it shook all the hangings on the walls. The dolls moved their arms and legs to the rhythm. The energy permeated her entire being. Her cells alive, her brain on fire.

Then darkness overtook her. She was thrown backward onto her heels. Total black. Total nothing.

CHAPTER 11

Mandy Rose had no idea how long she'd been "under." Her legs were caught beneath her and cramped painfully. She leaned over to free them. She was aware of the fact that she wore nothing beneath her muslin gown. She noticed several of the robed acolytes tilt their heads and lower their gaze to obtain a better view between her thighs. Ignoring her sense of modesty, she pulled her knees up to her chest one at a time in an effort to release the sharp pain behind her knees and in her calves. Somewhat relieved, she sat cross-legged, pulling the gown down over her folded legs.

A large person, gender indistinguishable, came over to her, quickly pulled her back onto her knees and growled, "Les genoux."

Mandy's knees quivered, so recently released from spasm but she obeyed, putting her hands on her thighs for bolstering. Her mind tumbled. *How long have I been here? Is this whole thing about me?*

She gaped up at the altar again and was taken aback. Not only was Clyde's gris-gris on that wall, it was the focal point. Candles had been lit and marched around the glass enclosure to caste a golden glimmer on the amulet. She marveled at the spectacle. No visible explanation for how those candles adhered to the wall.

A whining tone caught her attention. "Meh eh eh… meh eh eh." The goat. A goat.

What in God's name is a goat doing here?

The animal didn't seem too happy. It made sorrowful bleating noises and yanked on the red and white cord that tethered it to a lally column, almost hidden behind the candlelit altar. It was in a dark enough space that its eyes shone, two ruby red orbs. A picture of horror.

The monotonous drone of the chanting had a mesmerizing effect on Mandy. She weaved side to side, her knees becoming numb. The genderless giant being was once again touching her. She felt strong fingers pinching her shoulders from behind, keeping her from bending, keeping her ramrod straight.

The room swam before her eyes. She craved sleep, dreams, oblivion. A loud noise broke the spell. A drum pounded. *Ba boom, ba boom, ba boom.* A steady beat, like a pulse, a heart throbbing with unknown and terrifying dread. Strong bony fingers insulted her armpits, pushed into her and pulled her up.

Mandy was standing.

These same two sets of hands reached in unison to the hem of her gown. From behind her, they fetched the flimsy covering upward, halting a bit when the drums silenced. She didn't dare move, though the dress was covering her whole head. She could smell the dye in the material.

The drums resumed. The gown came off and was thrown toward the goat. The animal began nosing it, testing it to see if it was something good to eat.

Mandy Rose stood naked.

The drums accelerated. One long beat like an instrument with no hands, no humans, a life of its own.

A side door opened.

Two more no-gender beings entered. They held a litter. The passenger was a tiny, wrinkled woman. Her hair was fresh-snow white and billowed out around and behind her. She wore a square-necked frock of emerald green with garnet red trim. Her naked arms were little more than two pale bones that folded where the elbow connected the two parts. But her hands, oh her hands. They were impossibly narrow with fingers so long they resembled albino snakes. Each finger nail was shaved to a point and painted pure white that matched her hair. Her face was so shriveled it seemed a miracle any sound could be brought forth from a mouth so sunken it appeared to be devoid of lips.

The strange rickshaw stopped. The woman's eyes pierced Mandy Rose's face, then pointed one of those dagger-like fingers at her. The pencil thin mouth parted. "State your name."

Mandy's upper body trembled. She forgot all about using her acquired name of Bianca. "Um, Mandy. Uh, Mandy Rose."

The teeny woman leaned forward and continued. "Last name?"

"Uh, Bokum, Mandy Rose Bokum."

The ancient woman barked, "How do you come by Clyde Boudreaux's gris-gris?"

Mandy cringed. Her mouth fell open. She couldn't utter a word. The terror was so profound, her bladder let go. The warmth of her own urine provided a modicum of comfort.

"Speak young woman."

Mandy's vision blurred.

The old woman, the most venerated Voodoo priestess still alive, relented. "No harm will come to you. Answer me now."

Mandy took a deep breath and spoke. "Clyde Boudreaux is the father of my daughter."

"Why did you have his gris-gris?"

"I helped him to escape from the law and he left it with me."

"I repeat, why did you have it?"

Mandy Rose crumbled. "I'm sorry. I should've given it back to him."

The old woman's eyes slitted. "But you did not."

"I know. I was wrong. I wanted to learn about his religion and kept the gris-gris for its power."

A tiny beige tongue swung around the thin bottom lip, making it glisten. "You had no right. That totem was passed to him from his grandfather and is one of the, if not the, most power amulets in existence. You… young woman are nothing."

Mandy's head drooped low.

"Pick your head up right now. Where is Clyde?"

Mandy's spirits brightened, hoping this might redeem her. "Living at the house where I grew up."

The mother priestess glowered at Mandy. "Where is Clyde's daughter?"

"Hannah was kidnapped. She's returned now and living there also with her father."

"Kidnapped? How was that allowed to happen?"

Now Mandy Rose shrank into herself. Could this amazing magical woman tell Mandy was partially responsible for the taking of Hannah? The old woman narrowed her eyes again and ordered Mandy's removal to a predetermined room inside the building.

Mandy was speechless, too terrified even to cry out. She heard the loud calls from the acolytes. "Le sacrifice. Le sacrifice. Santeria. Santeria."

As she was led away, she was handed back her muslin gown and one of the handlers whispered to her, "They will now slit the goat's throat open. This is the ritual to keep your daughter Hannah and her father Clyde safe. You'll be brought a meal of the slain goat, which if you know what's good for you, you will eat every bit of. Leave no remains, not a single morsel."

Mandy managed a nod. She was amazed that this unknown person knew about Hannah and Clyde. She was a bit concerned about how this woman knew about them but dismissed the thought. What was happening? She should be very hungry, not having eaten any food for almost three days, but her gorge rose at what her next meal would likely consist of. Goat.

She peered back over her shoulder and saw a tall Black man leading the untethered goat to a wooden block where a petite white woman stood with a huge gleaming machete knife in her smallish hand. She was naked. There were blue bowls set in a circle around her and the site where the unlucky goat would draw its last breath.

"Le sacrifice."

<h1 style="text-align:center">CHAPTER 12</h1>

Mandy wondered if the goat, once slaughtered, would be eaten cooked or raw. A foul-tasting bubble rose from her stomach and lodged in her throat, making her voice sound strangled as she mumbled, "Oh my God." She focused on her herder. Again, she was at a loss to identify the gender. The "person" spun her through a doorway into a room no bigger than nine by twelve. The main furnishing was a double bed with a sumptuous quilt on it the color of a newly washed sky and piles of white pillows. She was told, "Lie down."

Mandy tried to grasp her gown from her captor, but the white knuckled hand held on. "Just lie down."

She did as she was told and curled into a tight little knot.

"Lie down flat, arms at your sides and legs spread."

Mandy listened to the voice, trying to determine if it was masculine or feminine.

"I won't hurt you."

She still couldn't tell a gender. She lay down and let her arms fall by her sides on the bed. There was a cloying smell of carnations.

She opened her legs. The person bent over her and said, "Close your eyes and relax."

Mandy tried to obey. She felt the mattress bend from the weight of the person who had brought her into this room. It looked like they were staying. She kept her eyes closed.

She felt a stiff finger between her legs. The finger slid up and down her inner lips. She spread her legs a bit more. Her fear lessened. She responded. She was also still terrified. Her emotions were confusing. But she succumbed to the pleasure. Would she be brought to climax so easily? She was ashamed of herself.

The finger kept on; sliding up and down, then into her to bring back silky moisture. Mandy was lost to what was happening to her. The clouds of pleasure billowed through her lower belly, down her thighs, and she heard herself squeal with delight. The hand that had brought her to such an exquisite climax now cupped her. Not a big hand.

Mandy opened her eyes and saw that it was a woman who'd just brought her to climax and done so in very little time. Her mind reeled. Is this lesbianism? *Am I now a lesbian?* No, not possible, but she now understood Cassandra's preference for sex with women. She blinked her eyes. The woman was watching her.

"I want to help, Mandy Rose. My name is Camille. She removed her turban, unwinding it from her head until she held a long thin dark blue scarf that had been folded long ways twice. Camille dropped the musk scented cloth across Mandy's thighs covering her most private parts.

Mandy wanted to trust her. She needed a confident, a friend. "Why do you want to help me?'

"I remember when I was just like you. I'd come by an amulet made of cloth. It depicted a horse having sex with a lady. They were copulating. It was said to have power to attract luck, love and sex. A talisman called 'Ma Sep Nang.' I claimed it as my own much as you have." Camille took in a breath. "But my dear, the laws are strict concerning ownership and 'jure sanguinis,' also called 'the right of blood.' It was discovered that I'd stolen the amulet from the rightful heir. This made for me a possible dangerous journey unless I could right the wrong and locate the correct heir, confess my sin and bring them here to the counsel." Camille stared into Mandy's eyes. "I've been informed Mandy, that you're now in that delicate position."

"Did you find the rightful heir and bring them here?"

"Ah, that's a tale you may not appreciate."

"Please tell me. I have to know. The gris-gris that was taken from me belongs to Clyde Bordeaux, given to him by his grandfather, who was lynched in front of Clyde when he was just a boy." Mandy's face contorted. She had completely returned to using her given name. The turn of events was sobering. She no longer wanted any part of calling herself Bianca.

"Correct me if I'm wrong, but you and Clyde have a child together?" With the question, a strange half-smile flashed across Camille's pretty face.

"Yes, a daughter. Hannah."

Once again, Mandy felt a hard to decipher darkness clutch at her chest. Again, she dismissed it. She needed this woman to be someone she could trust. Maybe, even a friend.

"My dear Mandy, Hannah is the rightful heir to that gris-gris. Does she know of its existence?"

Mandy pulled up on her elbow, completely comfortable, though still unclothed, with Camille and answered, "No, she's still young and only recently came to know Clyde as her father."

Camille touched her tongue to her top lip and continued. "As you may or may not know, it is the female who holds the most power in the Voodoo world. Your Hannah would take her place among the most venerated and authoritative forces, with power over all. She would rule.

"My amulet was of a lesser variety. The gris-gris you brought with you into New Orleans is extremely powerful and has the ability to be a source for great control and," now Camille dipped her head back a bit and said, "and evil. It is capable of influence in the highest of places. You were naïve to bring it here. Its energy is so potent with such magnitude its presence was felt by the highest priestesses. Therefore you were divested of it almost immediately upon your arrival. It became a matter of urgent concern; a powerful current was instantly felt."

"What do they want with me now?" Mandy's eyes rounded. "They have the gris-gris. They stole it from me right after I got here. They took it with great force, not gently."

Camille pushed her long silky hair back, then anchored it behind her elfin ears. "You must understand. The gris-gris is part of that bloodline. One of the three most influential bloodlines in history. And many believe of the three, it is the most powerful."

"Again, what do they want with me? What do they want from me?"

"They want Clyde Boudreaux in their clutches.

"But even more, they want Hannah."

CHAPTER 13

Arriona and Hannah sat in the back of the stretch limo; their school books on the seat between them. Cedric didn't "want" to listen to their conversation. The dividing glass slider wasn't closed all the way and the chauffeur found himself straining his ears to hear what the two girls were saying. It wasn't hard to differentiate who was speaking. Close in age, yes, but miles apart in personality. The plaintive voice of Arriona: "So what was it like with that adopted family in New Jersey?"

The clipped and authoritative voice was Hannah's. "Not like here, that's for sure."

"What was different?"

"Well Arriona, for one thing, we were learning French, and we had dinner parties with important people. I had dresses made especially for me out of the finest silks and woolens."

"Don't you like the dresses Gramma Sophie bought for you?"

Mouth twisting, Hannah replied, "Crap cotton, southern cotton. All very unsophisticated. Fine for a hick, which I am not."

Now Arriona's voice took on an edge. "I suppose you think I'm a hick?"

"Yes, I do. And a colored girl too."

"Hannah, you're half colored. Your father is a negro."

"Harumph! I do not for one minute believe that man is my father. Clyde, or whatever his name is."

The limo eased into the parking space in front of the private school specifically designed for the long low limousines. Cedric applied the brakes and exited through the driver's door. Very quickly he appeared at the door adjacent to the curb and pulled it open. The two girls grabbed their books and piled out. Arriona said, "Bye Cedric."

He responded, "Have a nice day, ladies. I'll be here to pick you up later."

Hannah mumbled, "Of course you will." She hugged her books to her chest and stormed off, heading for the elaborate entrance to the posh grammar school.

Arriona walked leisurely in the same direction.

<CENTER>**CHAPTER 14**</CENTER>

Angus leaned forward to concentrate on what Captain Richard Sloane was telling him.

Even with the office door closed, Rick was keeping his voice low, not wanting any of this to be common knowledge yet. "Angus, we all knew we had a long way to go to get these creeps. They have lotsa money to cover their tracks. New children are disappearing. Our task force is overwhelmed with calls. And we're hearing from neighboring states at an alarming rate since we're at the hub of this trafficking mess."

Angus's face looked gray and worn. Sophie'd told him he looked exhausted. His stomach contracted as his intestines made gurgling noises as he entertained very real thoughts of sharing with his wife what Captain Sloane was divulging. He queried, "What proof have we got?"

Rick answered as he pushed his hair back then checked his palm for sweat. A noisy "whew," escaped. "When we're sure we have enough facts to place some of our rescued kids, even the ones who were eventually sold to private families." Sloane paused.

"Go on, Captain… what?"

"I'm sorry Angus, some of these kids spent time as victims of sexual abuse."

"Where? Which kids?"

"Right here in Louisiana, happened before they were shipped out; mostly relocated up North."

Angus gritted his teeth and asked, "New Jersey?"

"I'm afraid so."

"How do we find out for sure?"

"Shit, Angus, they cover their asses. Again… money."

Angus knew Rick was disgusted. His nose had scrunched up as he used the atypical expletive.

Sloane said, "I'm gonna send Laura and Cassy out to pick the brains of our CIs. New cops have good luck with informants."

"Yeah, I know. I've seen that too."

Sloane continued. "Also, they're not known yet, no history; plus two women gathering information to help abused children is a recipe for success."

Angus knew better than to ask if Sloane thought this was a dangerous assignment. First of all, he knew it was. Secondly Laura and Cassy chose to be cops and were well aware of the dangers involved. More than once, informants and the cops they serviced met with deadly consequences.

"Okay, Captain. I'll tell them what their mission will be."

"Good Angus, the sooner the better."

Angus put his hands on his knees and pushed up off the wooden office chair that had seen finer days. His heart broke for Sophie. So much for her to bear. Mandy Rose missing. And now the possibility that little Hannah had been sexually abused as a very little girl. Angus thought of his mother, Pearl, and how she had strong religious beliefs; always saying God didn't give you any more than you could handle. What about this, Mama? A little girl, Mama. And adult men hurting her. Grown men, big men, Mama. A delicate innocent sweet little girl. Where was that God now, Mama?

CHAPTER 15

"Well Cassy, looks like we're up again."

"I don't think Angus wanted us out on the street yet. He's kind of paternal."

"You mean as in overprotective?" Laura smiled. "I know, but he has to accept reality. We're cops and take our assignments as they get handed to us by Sloane."

Also at the break room table, another rookie, a guy, was leaning sideways to tap into Laura and Cassy's conversation. The open box of doughnuts served as a means to get closer to the two women. He stood up, took a few steps and moved a metal chair aside, giving him room to reach into the open box for one of the two remaining offerings. Both plain crullers. "I overheard you two talking about going in the field for information on the missing kids?" Spoken as a question.

Cassy nodded. Laura just stared.

"Maybe I could be of help."

Cassy said, "Maybe."

"I was in on the early investigations. Name's Jensen; William Jensen. People call me Billy. I know you guys are Laura and Cassandra, also known as Cassy. You're both sort of famous." Billy directed his gaze to Laura. "You're Angus Clark's daughter, right?"

"Stepdaughter. It's possible you could be of help, Billy. Who did you talk to on the street that was helpful? Was it that homeless guy?"

"Guy's name was Weasel. His lady love is Maureen. Weasel told us what Maureen had told him. About that Big Carl. That's how he was tracked to the hotel he was staying at. He was one of the ring leaders shelling kids out for sex. He'd been a trafficker for over ten years. But, as you know, as soon as we put one of these bastards behind bars, two more crop up."

Laura's eyes drifted to one side for a second as she remembered her

37

mother taking Arriona to that hotel, hoping to be of help, and Arriona almost getting taken and raped by that piece of crap in his hotel room. Laura knew her tendency to be secretive, not open to help from others, trusting herself more. But this Billy seemed sincere; not looking for fame and glory.

"What do you suggest, Billy?"

Billy wormed in a little closer. "Weasel will be easy to find. Usually in Needle-town. Has his own hidey hole. Maureen moves around more. She's very tenderhearted where kids are concerned. Story is her twin daughters were taken from her by the state and put in the system. She's good at listening and picking up rumblings on the street."

Cassy and Laura exchanged a glance. Both had come to the same conclusion.

Cassy ventured, "Maybe you could be a third in this quest?"

Laura said, "Yeah, I'll run it by Angus this morning."

"I'm ready; don't have anything else pressing." Billy was full of admirable enthusiasm. Three hands reached to each other in a clasp that promised action and results. Three young cops, bold and eager.

What could possibly go wrong?

CHAPTER 16

Sophie mixed herself a very light drink. She'd discovered she could drink lemonade laced with vodka and no one panicked. Nobody accused her of "drinking" again. The tall skinny glass was frosty and the liquid an attractive pale yellow. She fingered the slice of lemon that floated on top. Twirling that golden citrus wedge helped her think. Or so she told herself.

There was no word on Mandy Rose's whereabouts. Clyde hadn't been home in two days. Was that good news or bad news? She loved having him live here, but her high hopes for him reaching Hannah were fading. Hannah was as cold as ice. The psychologists were failing her too.

Sophie plopped down in her club chair; the one embroidered with pink and aqua flowers. She traced one of the dark pink ones and took a long swallow of her cocktail.

Her yellow dress had shimmied up over her knees. With her wet lemony fingers, she pinched the adipose fat on the inside of her knee. She was getting fat again. She could still recall the nickname the cops gave her. So-fat Bokum. Another huge gulp and the elixir needed replenishing. She got up, headed for her hidden vodka stash. Her hand reached behind the seldom used stack of dishes, wiggling her fingers for the neck of the bottle.

Tap, tap, tap.

"Who could that be?"

Nobody was expected for hours. Even Almadine was gone till much later. She felt a bit tipsy, shook her head to clear the vertigo. She listened at the door. "Who's there?"

"It's me, Mrs. Clark. It's Cedric."

"Is anything wrong?"

"No, but please let me come in. I need to talk to you. It's important."

Sophie grabbed the handle and pushed the heavy door open. Cedric stood there, hat in hand and the face of someone in mourning. "Come in, Cedric. I've told you before, you don't have to knock."

"I know you have. Just habit."

"Come into the kitchen." Sophie and Cedric tramped into the kitchen, and Sophie said, "Sit down. I'll get you some lemonade."

Cedric seemed uncomfortable. He switched his hat to the other hand. Then back again. "No, no, thank you. No lemonade. I need to say what I've come to tell you."

"Cedric, you're scaring me. Are the girls okay? Was there an accident?"

"No, no accident, but it is about the girls."

Now he had her attention. "Please sit down."

He did.

Cedric twisted his jaw and swallowed.

"Okay, now please tell me what's upsetting you about the girls."

"It's about Hannah."

Sophie's stomach clenched and her mouth went dry. "Hannah! What about Hannah?"

"This is very hard to tell, ma'am."

"I see that. What are you afraid of?"

"I'm scared you won't believe me."

Sophie coughed; a dry raspy sound. Her breathing became noisy with wheezes.

Cedric jumped up and cried, "Where's your inhaler?"

"It's in my purse, on the counter. Please get it for me."

Cedric moved fast. Snapped open the large purse where the red inhaler sat in easy view. He snatched it and handed it to Sophie.

She tilted her head back as she shook the container that held her rescue solution.

While she administered the measured puffs of medication, Cedric dropped his hat and wrung his hands. He was having second thoughts about breaking silence concerning Hannah.

Sophie's breathing evened out as she lay the red inhaler down on the table, still clutched in her hand.

Cedric wanted to leave. "Are you okay, ma'am?"

"Yes, I'm better. Thank you. Please tell me what you came here to say."

Cedric's face paled, but he squared his shoulders. "Yes, ma'am."

Short pause. "I'm worried about Miss Hannah. Can you tell me if she was…" long pause, "…bothered by men, bad men, when she was gone missing?"

Sophie gasped, gripped her inhaler. "Why do you say that? What makes you say that?"

Cedric took a deep shuddering breath and said softly, "She reached into my lap, ma'am. She said in a whispery voice, 'I can make you happy.'"

"Oh my God. What did you do?"

"I lifted her hand and pushed it away. Then she said, 'I know how. I'm not just a little girl.'" Cedric had paled to the point where fainting was a distinct possibility.

Sophie said again, "Oh my God. My poor baby. What have they done to her?"

"I'm so sorry, ma'am."

Sophie looked at Cedric. A more miserable man she'd never seen in her life. She said, "You did the right thing. Don't tell anyone else. We will have to deal with this. I'm not sure how right now." Sophie took a big breath that was almost totally clear, thanks to the Albuterol.

She didn't doubt Cedric's disclosure.

Now she wanted Cedric to go so she could make a stronger lemonade.

CHAPTER 17

Mandy Rose and Camille were seated on the edge of the bed, holding hands when the door to the little room banged open. Two white-robed servers pushed a metal cart into the room. Both heads shaved bald; one vanilla colored bowling ball, one dark chocolate. The overhead light gleamed on them. Sweaty. Two sets of hands removed dome-shaped covers and revealed strips of seared meat, likely sizzling mere moments ago. There were apple slices soaked in cinnamon laid out in rows on a cream-colored platter that looked heavy and had tiny chips along the edges. There were no beverages and no utensils. Another bulky bowl held water where lemon slices floated and two cloth napkins peeked out from under it.

Camille rubbed her thumb on Mandy's knuckle and spoke for both of them. "We are honored to receive the sacrifice of the goat to feed the loa."

It was then Mandy Rose noticed the robes were not all white; there were bright red splotches and this same brilliant carmine was smeared all over the visitors' arms and necks. Good God, even their faces and bald heads. She gasped.

Camille clamped a hand over Mandy's lips, sealing any possibility of blurted words. She shot Mandy a sharp look.

Mandy shrugged her shoulders and after sucking her own lips in, managed to squeak out, "Yes, honored."

The two responded. They looked hard at Mandy and said in unison, "Madre de mambo." They bowed low and walked backward through the still open door. A hand reached in and grabbed the edge of the door and pulled it shut with a cracking sound; foreign for a door.

Mandy grimaced. "Oh my God. Is that the goat?"

"Yes and we better get eating. We'll be timed with no leeway. They want empty dishes and faces that show profound reverence and spiritual delight."

Mandy didn't argue. She ate.

42

CHAPTER 18

Later that evening, after the remains of the roasted goat dinner's odor faded, the two women talked. "How long do we have to stay here, Camille?"

"Hard to say. You're a special case."

"Tell me again why I'm special."

"The totem you had is considered one of the most powerful in existence. Did you not notice this while it was in your possession?"

Mandy didn't have to think too hard. She recalled it glowing on the floor of her car where Clyde had unknowingly dropped it. More than that, that totem thing had opened a heavy metal door in the cell of the mental facility where Clyde was locked up. She remembered the sound of a million bees and a shimmering energy that let the huge iron door just float open. After she relayed all this to Camille, she agreed to answer the question she had asked her earlier. She'd decided to trust Camille and sorely needed a friend.

"Okay, you want to know how they got the gris-gris away from me. I can't totally explain it; just know what happened. I was burrowed deep inside a leather booth at a nightclub and had the gris-gris tucked into a pocket of my pants; my front pocket where I kept it, so I could keep checking it was there. Through the front door came two monster size brutes. Both of them had heads like footballs, kind of pointy on top. I knew enough to be scared. They stood there without coming in. Those football heads swiveled in all directions. They kept their hands out and splayed like four massive radar screens. One of them whistled a high note. One continuous note. No melody. The other started a thrumming sound deep in his throat. The affect was mesmerizing. Some of the customers were tuned to it and stopped eating and drinking; gaping at the bruisers. Stranger still, some diners and music listeners appeared not to notice, didn't hear anything or find the two brutes noteworthy. Then a

43

third sound combined with the whistle and thrumming. A low-pitched keening; like a funeral wail. My pocket lit up. Their eyes bulged and lasered into my booth. They focused on my now alive and flashing pocket. In three long strides they were on me. They picked me up and pocketed the gris-gris in one swoop. I could swear they were afraid of Clyde's totem and also afraid of me. They carried me out that front door; being very gentle, but I knew I couldn't escape. I was so terrified I blacked out. The next thing I remember, I woke up in the room where they kept me before I was brought here. They took my shirt and pants and dressed me in this sack dress. I was alone in that awful room until coming here and the ceremony and then meeting you." Mandy exhaled as she finished.

"Wow, that gris-gris is fucking power-packed."

"I feel so dumb not to know much about any of this."

"You'll learn. They won't let you go."

"What do they want? I have no power."

"Yes, but you are linked with a true Receiver."

"You mean my lover? Clyde?"

"Yes."

Camille read the questioning look on Mandy's face and said, "I've been informed about you so I could help them accomplish what they want. They will stop at nothing to get what they want.

"They're looking for the next Mambo. This must be a female. They want one so powerful they can eliminate any enemies or adversaries to their agenda."

Mandy's face drooped. "What agenda?"

"Reviving the dead."

Mandy's hand shot up to her mouth and a strange gurgling sound erupted from deep within her. When at last she spoke, she said one word. One name.

"Hannah."

CHAPTER 19

"Laura, maybe we should start by interviewing the teenage boys who witnessed the abduction of the two sisters. Could be more to find out there."

Laura said, "Let's leave Billy out of this one."

Cassy's face clouded as she agreed. "I'm still not sure we should've included Billy at all."

Laura twisted her jaw, ignored Cassy's remark and said, "I have the name of their hangout. I'd like to make this less official and talk to them there on their turf."

"Agreed, let's go. Probably both there now."

The boys hung out where the tougher cliques spent their free time, which they all had way too much of.

The two cops in plain clothes pulled into a parking spot of a place so noisy you could hear the shouts of young males loaded with testosterone as soon as the car door opened. It looked small and in need of paint. The front door was slightly crooked; not enough hinges to keep it straight.

Laura and Cassy looked good for the visit. Cassy was dressed in a skin hugging black tube top and black jeans that clung to her long lean body. She'd finished the look with see-through plastic stiletto heels. Laura went with a short clingy red dress and red clogs. Heads turned. They drew every eye in the place.

Damn, what great luck. Their two quarries leaned on a counter; hips jutted out. The nearby pool table was seeing a lot of action. One player yelled, "Pow! You owe me. That game was mine."

Leon and Mike laughed at this outburst.

Laura and Cassy strode straight over to them, getting their attention at once.

"Well, what've we got here, ladies? To what do we owe this

unsolicited treat?" Leon did a double take at Mike's use of such a long word. He gulped. "Huh?"

Mike said, "Shut up, Leon."

The two women sidled up to them, getting closer than what was necessary. Near enough for the almost-men to smell the heady floral scent of freshly sprayed cologne.

Cassy said, "We'd like to talk to you and buy you a drink."

Mike punched Leon in the arm and said to Cassy, "Let's go."

The foursome found a booth where a single skinny blonde sat alone nursing a beer that'd long gone flat. Mike jerked his head her way and motioned with his thumb. She grabbed her stein and slid away, disappearing into the melee.

They sat down. The waitress was there in seconds. "What'll it be?"

Laura answered, "Four Sazeracs. That okay guys?" An approving nod was unanimous.

Mike said, as though he faced a microphone, "To what do we owe this pleasure?"

Cassy took the lead. "Don't freak. We're cops."

"Holy shit." Leon freaked.

Mike leaned in, his eyebrows raised, his face placid. "This about those two chicks?"

"Yeah, we're off-duty; wanted to see if you remembered anything that could help. We haven't found those girls yet. We know there's a kidnapping ring operating in this area."

"You mean, like for sex?"

"Yes, Mike. It's called human trafficking."

"I'll do anything I can to help. I have a little sister, and I'd kill anyone who took her to use her. Leon has two sisters."

"Yeah, that's right," Leon said over his initial reaction and eager to help. "I don't care about any reward no more. I do want to help catch those bastards."

The drinks arrived. Laura still wanted to sweeten the pot. How about some crab cakes to go with this? My treat."

Together the boys said, "Sure."

"Okay, I want you to go back in time to that afternoon. Did you see the girls first or the van?"

"We was ogling the girls. Is that the right word?"

"Yes. And then what?"

"Then the guy came with the puppy. He started fast talking to the girls. I was a little suspicious right away, 'cause he was old, yah know, like middle-aged and they was pretty young looking. They fell right for it with the puppy and all. The guy put the dog in the van and the smaller girl went right in after it, like to help it. The older girl might've hesitated a bit there, only for a second, 'cause he just shoved her right in and slammed the van's door shut there."

Laura took a sip of her Sazerac as the crabcakes arrived. She said, "Did the van look new or used like with worn tires or faded paint or anything you can recall?"

"The license plate wasn't clean. You could see it was like brown, sort of real dirty. The guy jumped in the passenger seat and the driver took off like a bat out of hell."

Laura cleared her throat, ahem. "Now Mike, Leon, would you be able to identify this guy if you looked at some photos?"

"You mean go down to the police station?"

"Yeah, could you do that?"

"I could," said Leon.

"Absolutely," said Mike.

Laura slapped down two cards and said, "If you think of anything or hear anything, call me. Day or night."

Mike said, "Like confidential informants?"

"Something like that," Cassy said as she pushed two of her cards across the table also.

"We need to go, Laura. I want to see Arriona before she goes to bed"

"Okay, so guys, I'll pay the tab on my way out and spring for seconds on everything."

The boys tried to hide their smiles but failed.

The two women slid out of the bench seat and headed for the cash register.

Cassy took a glance back at the two young men who appeared to be in serious conversation. They'd split up so as not to be seen sitting together on the same side of the booth.

Both women felt the meeting might prove helpful. Or not.

<h1 style="text-align:center">CHAPTER 20</h1>

Clyde never could help himself. He was a woman magnet. Mimi was no exception. But there was something else about her. An air of secrecy. More to her. She had a hidden agenda. There was something afoot more than a roll in the hay with him. She wanted to go to a different club. He saw no reason to do that; but no reason not to, so he acquiesced.

"Do you have a car?"

Mimi shook her head.

Clyde put his hand on the small of her back, enjoyed the tightness of the muscles there and led her to the T-Bird.

"Wow!" Big smile. "Nice ride."

"It belongs to the woman I'm trying to find."

Mimi's head jerked back a bit even though Clyde suspected this wasn't news to her.

"C'mon honey. I'll show you the bar I want. You'll love it."

Clyde agreed. "Okay with me."

It was only two streets away, but the area seemed darker and somehow malevolent. Clyde noted street lights were missing; maybe broken by vandals? He parked the car, locked it and they got out in front of the place Mimi pointed at. The dark green door was barely visible in the poor light. There was broken glass on the sidewalk as they headed to the entrance, causing them to weave left and right, avoiding punctures to shoes not meant for abuse. Mimi knew the peculiar knock was private and needed to be used to be admitted. Her skinny knuckles tapped twice, waited for a count of three, then three more. *Rap, rap*, pause, *rap, rap, rap*. The door creaked as it opened, letting yellow light spill out onto the street. The beam illuminated two faces requesting admittance.

No sooner had they stepped inside than Clyde decided he'd been shanghaied. Mimi separated herself from him as two mammoth bruisers jerked his arms so hard he feared one or both would leave their sockets. He narrowed his eyes and glared at his new "friend" Mimi.

She refused to meet his gaze.

"Okay boy, we're not gonna hurt you. Just want some information."

Clyde jutted his jaw and proclaimed, "I want information too. I'm looking for a girl. She's petite and has most of the hair cut off her head."

The smaller of the two giants smiled, showing a gap in his lower teeth, but still managed to look pleased. He said, "Is that girl related to you?"

Clyde took that as truth they knew about Mandy Rose. He countered with, "Why? Do you know where she is?"

The guy whose name was Bull said, "We ask the questions here. What is that girl to you?"

Clyde's right arm was now torqued up behind his back, causing excruciating pain. His other arm was immobile due to the other brute holding it aloft and not too gently.

Clyde knew he was bested. "Ow, all right. Let go. Fucking let go. I'll answer. That girl is, was, my woman. We have a daughter together."

Bull yelled, "Bingo."

Clyde tried again. "Can you answer me now about her? Where she is?"

Bull took a deep breath, said simply, "She's safe, in good hands."

Clyde roared. "Safe? Safe from what? From who?"

Bull sat down on a dirty ottoman all business-like and queried Clyde some more. "Are you aware this girl had the gris-gris that was bequeathed to you from your grandfather?"

Clyde saw no way out, so he answered, "I assumed that's where it went. She was with me when it went missing."

"That girl does not harness the power. There is no bloodline."

"Yeah, so what's that to you?"

"Everything! We have the gris-gris in our possession now."

"But it belongs to me." Clyde was shouting.

"That was only temporary."

"What the hell do you mean?"

"Temporary until the next female in the bloodline could take possession and as the effeminate master, explode its power to seize control over the people under its jurisdiction."

Still yelling, Clyde barked, "That power belongs to me."

"You, being male, cannot bring it to its apex."

Clyde tried to explain. "My woman, Mandy Rose, helped me use its power to escape a locked dungeon in a mental facility. Something never done before."

"That's all well and good, but now Mambo wants more. She needs a replacement as her years are many, and she has much to teach the next in line for the crown of ultimate Voodoo power."

Clyde's face shrank as comprehension made itself known in his mind. He realized who they were talking about as the "replacement." "You stay away from my daughter. She's still very young."

"She's the perfect age. She may already be aware of her destiny."

Clyde's neck prickled as he recalled Sophie's confusion about the chants heard coming from Hannah's bedroom. She called the sounds eerie; said the words were none she recognized. When asked about it, Hannah denied it ever happened.

Sophie said, "I was afraid for her and told her so."

Hannah just smiled."

CHAPTER 21

Sophie fortified herself with her favorite mixture. Gin and lemonade. She sat at the kitchen table in the sunroom. The late day sun; now totally blocked. Lately she preferred darkness. She wasn't thrilled with her puffy eyes and blotchy skin. She laid in wait for Laura and Cassy to arrive. The grandmother of Hannah swirled the slice of lemon two and a half times and stared into middle distance. She heard Hannah and Arriona in the bedroom down the hall talking; no arguing. The dominant voice was Hannah's. Arriona sounded placating, plaintive; but not whiney. Sophie dropped her head into her hands, one fist still grasping the drippy glass of doctored lemonade.

A noisy clamber announced the two young women. They went straight to the kitchen and dropped their carry-ons on the table.

Laura's eyes were hard. "Mama, what're you doing? What's wrong?"

Sophie shushed her, one wet finger to her swollen lips. "Girls, we have to talk."

Cassy said, "Me too?"

"Yes, you too. Sit."

Happy for a sit-down, they plopped into the empty chairs and waited for Sophie to continue.

"Do you want some lemonade? Are you thirsty?"

"No, Mama. Later. Just tell us what's troubling you."

Cassy piped up. "We sort of already have an idea."

Sophie took a long drought and put her glass down, finally letting go of it. "I'm worried about Hannah. Nothing is working. She's angry all the time. She's abusive toward Arriona."

Cassy nodded at this disclosure.

Sophie went on. "And Cedric told me a story today; a very disturbing story."

The two young women leaned in closer, instinctively knowing voices must be discrete.

51

Sophie picked up her empty glass and put it down again. "Okay, here it is. Cedric told me Hannah behaved provocatively toward him."

"No!" from Laura.

"Yeah. I'm deeply concerned about the time span between when she was taken and when she was sent to New Jersey to her adoptive family."

Laura fumed. Her face red and rigid. And her damned sister missing. Again! *And now Clyde!* Some parents! *This family is doomed.* Laura let out a puff of breath. "Oh, Mama."

Cassy put her hand on Laura's shoulder. "Try not to imagine the worst. Let's continue with our investigation about the missing kids and see what's true and what isn't."

"What time is Angus coming home, Ma?"

Sophie paled at the mention of Angus. "Maybe an hour, maybe less. Almadine plans dinner for seven."

Laura, in control again, said, "Okay, we'll have a meeting tonight after Hannah and Arriona are in bed."

All heads turned as a higher-pitched voice demanded, "What's happening after we're in bed?" The words *we're in bed* were spoken sharply, full of accusation. Hannah strode to the table and plunked folded fists down on it. She eyeballed each adult and announced crisply, "If you're planning to discuss me, I want to be here."

A shocked silence ensued.

"Hannah honey, we don't want to keep you awake. It's just about house stuff."

Her eyes were slits. "Do you think I'm stupid, 'Gramma'?" That last word spoken with undisguised venom. Tears rolled down Sophie's cheeks, but Hannah wasn't finished. "And, don't think we don't know your 'lemon aid' is half booze."

Laura shouted, "Hannah, that's enough."

Arriona swept in, taking Hannah by the elbow, murmuring practiced soothing phrases. "C'mon Hannah, ease up for now. Let's go and listen to that new AC/DC we just got."

Hannah conceded, let Arriona lead her away but could be heard saying, "Okay, goody two shoes."

Laura lamented, "Oh, there's definitely more of a problem here than we anticipated. I'm hoping uncovering more of the facts we can look for more of a healing for our little Hannah."

Sophie and Cassy only nodded without conviction.

CHAPTER 22

"Do you think that delinquent Mike had a change of heart and wants to help find these creeps?" Cassy asked Laura.

"I doubt it. He's still Jonesing for reward money. That's okay. He might dig something up that we want."

"You're probably right. Where're we picking Billy up?"

Laura twisted her jaw before she answered, "I still have reservations about that guy. Not 'cause he's a rookie, but because he's a bit too eager. Too confident. Plus, if something goes bad, we have to trust him to keep his mouth shut."

Proving Cassy's point, Billy Jensen was standing on the sidewalk in front of his apartment building. Laura'd hoped they would've gone in to get him, had the chance to see his digs, give them a feel for how he lived, who he was. The cruiser never came to a full stop before Billy had the back seat door open. Out of breath from exuberance, he slid in and barked, "Let's go."

Cassy turned from the shotgun seat and said to Billy, "We're starting with Needle-town. We know a few stoolies that bunk there."

"Names?"

"One is Weasel, probably our best bet."

Billy's eyes brightened.

"Yep, as I've said before, I know this guy well. I went to his hidey-hole with Cartwright Spencer. Guy likes cash and cigarettes."

Cassy reached down by her feet and swung up a whole carton of Marlboros.

Billy chuckled. "Marlboros. Wow, that's gold. Weasel will be thrilled and talkative."

Laura jutted her chin back at Jensen and said, "Billy, let me and Cass do the talking at first. You can round it up for the kill."

"Right on."

Laura and Cassy exchanged a *told you so* look at the right on remark. Conversation died off until they reached their destination.

Laura pulled in to the edge of the encampment; too dangerous getting too close. There would be transient dwellers rolled up in makeshift bed rolls, lying in no particular order on the ground.

They left the car and picked their way gingerly into where Weasel made his home. His cardboard box bungalow still had the drape Billy remembered. These afforded Weasel his version of privacy.

As they got closer, they heard giggles, feminine giggles, coming from the box's interior. Outside on the ground was a well-worn pair of high-top sneakers with the remnants of what used to be pink shoe laces. Weasel's faded argyle socks were folded over a nearby bush. Next to them was a gone-gray pair of tighty-whiteys.

Laura said, "Must've interrupted laundry day."

Cassy said, "Shit, he's got company."

Billy said in a too-loud voice, "Weasel." Before he got another word out, Laura gave him an ice-cold glare that froze his tonsils. He shut his mouth.

The chatter in the box stopped. Some rummaging around noises spoke of garment gathering and modesty being observed. The trio of cops waited.

"You stay here, Maureen. I'll take care of this."

Weasel's head popped out. His abundant hair scrambled in three directions. As though he had a mirror in front of him, he clawed his fingers through his unruly mop. The hair lined up nicely. He pushed out in full view; his eyes shiny as they located the carton of Marlboros tucked under Cassy's arm.

"What's up guys? Hey, I remember you," he said as he zeroed in on Billy.

"Hi Weasel. This is Laura and the gal with the cigarettes is Cassy."

Weasel waved his hand, palm out; a politician catering to his followers. His face a blank.

The cops squatted to be eye level with Weasel. Weasel felt very important. He waited though.

"We're looking again for information about kids. Kids taken and maybe trafficked."

"I know what that means." Old Weasel *in the know*. He answered, "I can help you some."

"How? How're you gonna help us."

Cassy lifted her elbow; the cigarettes dropped to the ground. Weasel snatched them up and passed the carton back into the box.

"What else you got for me?"

"Depends what you tell us and then depends if it helps."

"Awright. I heard somebody from the camp here say there was a white van that took some kids, mostly girls… to a place where there were more girls."

"Be specific, Weasel. We're not here to play games." Laura wanted answers.

"No games. There's a factory. Not sure which one, but it's where they used to store lumber. One of those buildings next to the old electric plant."

"You mean on Bay Street?"

"Think so. Yeah, Bay Street."

"Where'd you get this info?"

"Maureen told it to me." Upon hearing her name, she put one slender-fingered hand out to rest on Weasel's shoulder and pushed it gently to one side so she could join the discussion. An attractive lilting voice said, "Yes, I heard that being talked about when I was downtown."

"C'mon out here, Maureen. You were very helpful once before. Because of your intel, we captured one of the big bosses in the trafficking ring"

Maureen looked at Laura and ventured a guess. "Were you related to that little girl that was taken?"

"Yes, her name's Hannah. She's my niece."

"Is she home and okay now?"

"She's home. We want to find out more about where she was kept."

Maureen shook her head and said, "They had some little girls at an old Girl Scout camp." Pause. "Some little boys also."

Maureen had an educated air about her. Laura and Cassy wondered what'd happened in her life to make her end up having sex in a cardboard box in Needle-town.

Weasel felt left out. "So is this stuff helpful?"

Cassy drew two ten-dollar bills from her pocket and handed one to Weasel and one to Maureen.

Laura reached into a watch pocket and extracted an almost new red lipstick and held it out for Maureen to accept or reject.

"May I see the shade?"

Laura pushed the pinkish-red lipstick up for inspection.

"Yes, that's a good color for me. Thank you." Maureen took it with two fingers, pinky held aloft.

Billy wanted airtime. He said, "We'll be back to see if you find out anything else to help us. Keep your eyes and ears open, but play it safe. These are bad guys."

After goodbyes, the trio left and the happy couple returned to their conjugal visit in the box.

Once they were on the road again, Billy said, "I know where that old Girl Scout camp is. These guys are pretty ballsy staying in the same area."

Laura and Cassy were deep in thought.

Cassy spoke first. "Let's go there right now."

"Now. Without backup?"

"Yes, Billy" said Laura. "Right now."

CHAPTER 23

"Hey girls, shouldn't we let someone know what we're doing?"

Cassy leaned on the back of her seat, twisted her head to stare directly at Billy. He was hunched forward and not looking too happy.

"Cool down 'boy,' we're only gonna take a peek, not doing a takedown. Gotta make sure Weasel and Maureen's intel is accurate. Waste less time this way. Understand?"

"Oh… yeah, guess I see the sense in corroboration. Maybe it's creepy old buildings full of cobwebs and rat shit. Right?" Billy's young body folded a bit as he relaxed.

The buildings came into view. Suspicious was the fact that there were vehicles parked alongside of the main building. Two of these were vans. Neither was white. The other vehicle was a sleek black elegant-looking car. Billy yelled, "Shit, that's a New Yorker. Costs all of our yearly salaries combined."

Laura ignored Billy's exuberance. "We've hit pay dirt."

Cassy added, "We need to get a look in those windows."

Billy's body stiffened.

Laura tooled right past the clump of old structures; pulled into a small grove of trees across the street with copious Spanish moss dripping down affording good cover. "We wait here till it's dark. Any objections?"

Cassy said, "Agreed."

Billy said, "Okay, but I have to take a piss."

"Jesus Christ, Billy. You don't need permission."

The sound of another vehicle. Before Billy could get the door open, all talk ceased.

Another van rolled in next to the two parked there. The cops' vision was partially obscured but gave enough of a view through the branches to watch for whatever happened next.

The front door of the main building opened. Two large men

erupted. They laughed and gestured as though they were guests at a bawdy afternoon party. One had a hip flask protruding from his back pocket. This got a loving pat as he shuffled to the van. The other brute took a ring of keys from his belt and unlocked the van's back door. Both men were bent at their waists as they reached into the dark interior of the van. Windows were blacked out somehow and appeared as solid dead squares.

What they pulled out of the recesses was shocking. A reality too hideous to comprehend.

The children all appeared drugged. The muscular biceps of the heartless butchers easily held one child in each arm. They carried four total at once. Skinny legs dangled down, banging against the side of the pitiless fiends. One child was missing a shoe, another had white socks on for this merciless journey.

What must their parents be going through right now?

The Goliath brutes never stopped kidding around. They trundled all four little ones into the building. The van door hung open, waiting. Task not finished, the flask toting monster went back, reached in and pulled out one more little one, possibly a boy, indicated by long brown pants and high-top sneakers.

He was carried into the building and added to the human pile of sorrow. Five children destined for what? Were they being trafficked? Used for sex? Sex forced on their innocence by deviants; some of whom were excited by cruelty. Were other children already being held in there? Were they drugged and was that more merciful? There were no good answers. This was what Laura and Cassy had signed up for. Billy too was now ensnared in this heart-wrenching mission.

They whispered, though they wouldn't have been heard. It felt unseemly to speak in a normal tone of voice. Like when you enter a house where the family's baby just died.

Billy rasped, "What do we do now?"

"We have enough proof to do an entry and arrest at least for kidnapping. This appears to not be a one-time occurrence. We have to run it by Sloane. Get Angus involved too."

"Yeah, but Cassy, we don't know if this is a holding place or if sexual assault crimes are taking place here."

Billy found his voice. "I want to stop this fast before those kids we just saw get manhandled and used by those creepy pieces of shit."

Cassy said, "If we want to stay to find out, that means leaving those kids in there for who knows how long."

Laura answered, "Give me twenty minutes to see inside that building, then we call headquarters."

"That's dangerous."

"I know, Cass. I'll be careful."

"Twenty minutes, then we call Sloane."

Billy sat open-mouthed. His brain on overload. He couldn't agree to this Maverick move but knew he was outnumbered. He didn't bother to vote.

CHAPTER 24

Laura took a swig from the plastic bottle of spring water then tucked her shirt into the front of her pants; left the back loose to cover her little Beretta, which she patted. Cassy's eyes were wide and wet, but she knew her good friend's mind was made up. Billy's face was a mixture of fear and respect.

He said, "Take the Rover, Laura, and call if you need us."

"No, it's too bulky. I won't be long. Ten minutes… fifteen tops."

Twenty seconds later Laura could smell the damp earth beneath her nostrils as she wormed her way over to the building suspected of being the worst kind of brothel. Her elbows took the brunt of the journey. She stretched her head up to gauge her progress. The closer she got to her objective the faster her heart sped up. Her spit disappeared in her mouth. She heard her own huffing and puffing as her breathing became ragged.

Loud voices. "Oh, shit." Her head butted against the stone building. She sucked her legs up into her chest, making herself as small as possible.

Coarse laughter from low-pitched voices. Men's garrulous guffawing, the tone licentious and evil.

She plastered herself to the wall and smoothed her hair down so none stuck up, catching a breeze. She stayed stuck to the bricks, sliding along inch by inch, ignoring the gathering cramp in her calf. A filthy window two feet up. She went on her knees and peeked through. Glad it was so dirty.

The room was full. A den of depraved and rotten wickedness. The window revealed grown men milling around. One person seated, a gray-haired woman, half glasses perched low on her nose, taking down notes of some kind.

The children were the featured attraction.

The four little girls were standing on a long table. Their clothing had been taken away from them. Their eyes darted all over the walls and ceiling. Each little face was shiny with tears.

They were being inspected by some of the men in the room. All of whom were fully clothed. A door opened and a very large red-haired woman marched in pushing the little boy from the van. He looked around himself and bolted his chin, trying to twist away from her. She had big meaty fingers pinching the back of his neck, keeping him moving now on his toes. Reprisal was swift. Her free hand slapped his youthful face and shoved him forward. Then she pointed at the display table.

One of the men lifted him from under his naked armpits and forced him to sit on the edge of the table. He directed the boy to spread his knees. The men hooted and hollered their approval. The boy's head dropped to his chest.

Now the bargaining would begin. The big woman walked over to the little dark-haired girl who'd somehow managed to still have her vision-correcting glasses on. The giantess snatched the glasses and slapped her hand on top of the pint-sized head.

It's an auction. Jesus Christ. It's an auction. Laura's gorge rose, spewing a teaspoon of vomit into her mouth.

The gray-hair demoness was the auctioneer. "How much for this little darling? She's about seven years old. Will last a good long time."

One brute barked out, "Six hundred."

Laura'd seen and heard enough. This was a place where children were sold. Sold to traffickers or pimps. She clamped her hand across her mouth to stifle the urge to vomit. To throw up what she'd witnessed. Now to make it back to the car, beg for backup and an immediate sting operation to stop this now. She curled around, reversed her journey.

Elbows raw and bleeding, she put on a burst of speed and staying low, aimed toward the car.

A voice broke through. It was loud. "Hey, someone's out there. I'll get 'em." On the run came a huge bruiser of a man. Big clodhopper boots made humungous strides.

"Ping." Laura was getting shot at.

"Shit. I gotta shoot this bastard."

Laura bellied over and pulled out her Beretta, happy for all the time she spent at the department's shooting gallery. Confident, she leaned her shooting arm on her forearm and fired three times. *Bang, bang, bang.*

With a surprised look on his ugly mug, the big guy stopped. He lifted his pistol toward Laura, aiming for her head. *Bang.* Again she fired. He toppled over like a redwood, his gun hand getting buried under his bulk. The heap lay still.

Now the sound of an engine filled her almost deafened ears. The black and white skidded up alongside her in the field. The door flew open and Billy jumped out. He half-carried, half-dragged her, forced her into the back seat, all the while saying, "You're okay, you're okay."

Cassy roared off, spraying dirt and pebbles into the hot air.

The field they'd just left was now peopled with other miscreants, all armed and looking for blood.

Cassy was an ace driver; knew right where she was headed. Billy could see that one of the vans was rolling out of the parking space.

"Are you all right, Laura?"

"I'm fine. Just drive. Start the lights and siren."

Billy was bug-eyed. This was more than he could've ever hoped for. In the shotgun seat, keeping low, he had his revolver out and watched behind them. The van was in his sight; it leaned left and right, not stable. An arm reached out of the passenger seat and a flash of light came from the shiny thing in their hand. The van wobbled wildly. Another shot and holy shit. The van couldn't make the corner, not at that speed. It flipped over on its side and continued to roll.

People, probably a picnicking family, on the adjacent lawn scrambled; ran in all directions to save themselves and give the runaway van room to destroy itself.

Ka-boom. Red, yellow and blue flames escaped; a life snuffing explosion. No one would survive.

Billy was on his Rover reporting the accident, still aware not all of the criminals were in that van. He also announced their previous activities and requested several squads and two ambulances be sent to the site they'd just left. Underneath, his mind unscrambled all that'd just transpired. He figured they were all in deep trouble. And Laura had shot a man. Most likely killed him.

Cassy and Laura were also replaying the events of the last few hours. Would they lose their badges?

Too soon for comfort, the precinct came into view. They entered at a normal speed, pulled into the lot and parked the car. Nobody moved. They sat. Still and stony-faced.

Laura came alive first. "Let's go, gang. Can't put this off."

Faces turned toward the trio. Word had spread.

CHAPTER 25

Clyde tried again. Maybe he could reason with these animals. "My daughter hasn't reached puberty. She's a child."

The crude men exchanged a knowing look that made Clyde's blood run cold. A roaring sound started in his head. His thoughts congealed. "What do these men want?"

Clyde looked at Mimi, now pouring herself a tall glass of some type of clear liquid. He'd never seen a bottle like the one she held aloft. A skull. A glass skull with a spout. Not ready to give up, he said, "I'm the one who owns…" He paused, knowing he couldn't claim ownership since these beasts now had, probably hidden somewhere, his gris-gris. This was his most valuable possession. If he'd gotten to Mandy Rose first, it would still be his. Rightfully his. Damn it. He felt nauseous, bowels noisily turning to swill.

The man wearing a turban barked, "Lock him up. Put him in a cell."

The one with the Atlas build, obviously in charge, put up a hand in the stop position. "No, he goes free. He'll lead us to the girl."

Clyde felt sicker. What was he gonna do? He couldn't let them follow him to the mansion, wouldn't let them find Hannah. He knew what their agenda was now. She was the raw material. The rightful heiress of the most powerful Voodoo magic in existence.

But what about Hannah? How much energy was passed down genetically? Clyde knew at an early age his grandfather had bequeathed him not only the physical gris-gris and the energy contained in the amulet but also the consciousness of it. But more important; the passing on of the DNA, which would come to full capacity only in a female. This could not be denied.

He couldn't go home yet. He had to find Mandy Rose. Had to find Hannah's mama.

He found himself being shoved toward the door. Two men, both

63

bigger than he was, held him by his upper arms and with no pretense of civility, pushed him through the open doorway. One man lifted his foot and crammed it into Clyde's lower back so hard he feared his spinal cord might snap.

Sprawled out on a damp concrete apron, he imagined he saw Hannah. In the vision, she wore a hooded cloak of deep burgundy. She showed him her palms. Her enigmatic smile was a mixture of familial compassion and pure evil. He was torn asunder. He loved his daughter, but his limbs trembled with icy fear.

CHAPTER 26

The threesome exited the police car. They dragged their feet heading into the precinct. Billy and Cassy made it through the door first. Laura backhanded the sweat from her forehead and tightened her spine. Her chin was up and her stride was long. The squad room silenced. All heads swiveled to catch a glimpse of the rookies who'd just murdered a perp.

Angus's face was red and shiny. He came sideways out of the doorway used for a war room. He felt no need to walk all the way into the tension-filled outer room. One wave on his arm gestured into the inner sanctum.

Laura had never seen her gentle, grace under pressure, stepfather looking so pissed. She took the lead going into the room, accustomed to strife, pain and misery. Billy and Cassy hung behind, prolonging the inevitable. Angus addressed them with a surly, "You two also. Get in here."

The squad room still held its tongue. This was big. A brand new cop, a rookie, according to the report, shot a guy. Shot him several times; left him dead for the bus to pick his body up. Should've been the cadaver wagon; the guy was dead as dead can be. Shot by Laura Bokum.

Inside the war room, Angus stood, both hands planted on the six-foot gray table.

His eyes threw sparks.

He said, "Sit."

Three chairs scraped and scratched until three bottoms were parked. Laura started. "Angus, it was self-defense."

"Quiet." Angus looked directly at Billy. "What happened, Officer Jensen. What did you see?"

"Uh, it's like Laura said. The man burst out of the building we were watching. They were holding kids, looked like an auction. The kids were naked."

Angus pounded the table. "Tell me about the shooting. Save the details."

Billy took a stuttering breath. "Uh, uh." Then began again. "He."

"He, who?"

"Uh, the man that got shot, got killed."

"Did you check to see if he was dead?"

"No, but—"

"Then stick to what you saw."

Billy looked down and tried for a third time. "The man came out of the building and started shooting. Laura was on her belly on the ground moving away and in the line of fire. She turned to face the shooter and pulled out her own gun and returned fire."

"How many times did she shoot?"

"Three or four."

"Was the man still firing?

"Uh, I think so."

"How many times did he fire?"

"More than once. I know that."

"Then what?"

"We started the vehicle and sped to where Laura was on the grass. I pushed her into the back seat."

"When did you call for the ambulance?"

"Right then, from the car."

Angus moved his jaw side to side. "When did you decide you didn't need backup approaching a dangerous, possibly deadly situation?"

"Um, we should've called earlier."

"When should you've called?"

"Before Laura went up to that building."

"You're God damned right. Before Laura went up to that building."

Cassy bit her lower lip but refused to look at Laura. Angus moved his focus to Cassy now. "What can you add?"

"It's just like officer Jensen said. The guy came out shooting. Laura defended herself."

Angus let the energy in the room simmer down a bit. Some of the beet color left his cheeks. A minute passed while no one spoke.

"Laura, what've you got to say?"

She breathed heavily in and out. Heard a rasp and thought for a second, Hope I'm not getting my mother's asthma. "I was wrong to pull a stunt like that. I let my emotions rule my intellect. I'm lucky I'm not in the morgue right now. I deserve whatever happens."

Angus, much calmer, said, "It was a rookie boner. All three of you were acting on adrenaline, forgetting the basics. This is why we have these rules. Also why we lose good men who act with good intentions but are foolhardy." He ground Laura into a pulp with his hard-boiled eyes and spat, "And good women too."

Laura took it without complaint, keeping her face penitent. Angus was right. They were all wrong. Mostly me, she thought.

Angus wiped the corner of his mouth and said evenly, "This will go before internal affairs of course. It may be deemed a 'good shooting.' But as of now your behavior necessitates turning in your badges. And your firearms. This is far from over."

Angus pointed to Captain Sloane's office, and they all trailed over there. The captain stood when they entered. He moved his green blotter out to the edge of his desk and slapped his right palm over it. Rick Sloane's face was drawn up in pain, his handsome features masked.

Cassy dropped her badge and pistol on the blotter and Billy followed. Laura's head tilted to one side, not wanting the full picture of her gun lying there next to Cassy and Billy's and her beautiful badge she'd worked so hard for dumped like so much junk as she did as she was told.

"You're all dismissed. Angus will let you know when your depositions will be held. Laura, you'll go before a full board as is the policy for a shooting resulting in death of an individual."

There were three, "Yes, sirs."

The office was emptied except for Captain Richard Sloane. He put his chin in his hand and ogled the three pistols and badges. He closed his eyes and shook his head in slow motion.

CHAPTER 27

Clyde's mouth filled with the taste of copper. His own blood. He recalled learning somewhere that tongues heal on their own. Still hurt like a bitch. With both of his arms pinned behind him by those brutes, he couldn't break his fall. He was happy those two gorillas closed the door behind them after they finished catapulting Clyde onto the dirty sidewalk. He'd no desire to be observed. He folded himself into a seated position. His chin and knees had taken a shellacking. Not to mention his poor tongue. But not as bad as the beating he'd taken in Mexico. He used his unscraped hands to push himself up. Took one last look at the door he was just flung out of.

Now his mind turned to Mandy Rose and Hannah. He was desperate to find Mandy. They had to protect their little girl. He still had a personal relationship with that amulet. It was his juju. His to command.

His head drooped to one side. He spit some blood mixed saliva, then limped down the darkened street. Darker thoughts swirled. None of this would've happened if his gris-gris wasn't separated from him. His grandfather would be aghast if he knew that the gris-gris entrusted to Clyde was not in his possession.

That powerful force belonged with him. It was his. The omnipotence it bestowed must be returned home. Home to him.

Then and only then would a line of heritage, a birthright legacy, be carried out as proclaimed by the elders.

Little Hannah would be the recipient of this most powerful endowment.

First, he must find Mandy Rose.

CHAPTER 28

"I never would've thought goat could taste so good. Didn't realize I was so hungry."

Camille's lips were shiny from the fat on the edges of the roasted goat chops. She nodded in agreement, then said, "How invested are you in becoming a Voodoo follower? One with full membership."

Mandy tucked her legs underneath her butt and leaned her elbows on her knees before she answered, "I'm very confused. I wanted to explore the path and felt like I had an advantage 'cause I had Clyde's gris-gris. Now they took it from me. I'm like a prisoner. I'm nothing. I don't have the amulet. I'm not sure if Clyde is here in New Orleans looking for me or if he hates me." Her eyes glistened. "It's my fault the gris-gris is out of our hands. And," a tear popped from one eye, "I can't even think about Hannah. I've been a crap mother. I allowed her to be kidnapped. I never stayed to be there when she came back home. I'm weak. I hate myself."

Camille's eyes widened. "You let your daughter be kidnapped?"

"Yes, I overheard my father making plans on the phone. I did nothing to stop it."

"Christ, Mandy. Where's your daughter now?"

"With my mother. Maybe with Clyde… her father."

"Where's your father?"

"My father was a pedophile piece of shit. He molested me over and over. And scores of other little girls. He was instrumental in a sex trafficking ring."

"And now?"

"Dead. Someone knifed the bastard in prison."

"Okay, all in the past. What're you gonna do now?"

In a quiet voice, Mandy answered, "I'm not seeing too many choices. Will these people hold me here forever? Am I their captive?"

69

"Hard to say. They've tasked me with keeping you available."

"Available for what?"

Camille looked down. "Whatever needs of theirs you can fulfill. And more importantly, you're a conduit to your daughter, Hannah, whom they want."

Mandy produced a tortured sigh that had a grasping sound to it. She held her head in her hands. Deep sadness caused her body to rock back and forth. Her eyes stared and remained desert dry.

Camille watched the broken woman and was torn in her feelings.

CHAPTER 29

Laura needed to talk to Clyde.

Being at the breakfast table late in the morning felt weird. No job. No school. She studied the plate Almadine had set before her over half an hour ago. The orange-colored eggs had congealed and had even less appeal than before. The coffee pot requested by her got her attention. She poured her fourth cup and plunked in three sugar cubes. The creamer gave up its last few drops, barely lightening the now black as prune juice java.

Sophie scuffled over to her daughter and laid her hands on Laura's shoulders. "Not hungry?"

"No, Ma."

"How're you feeling?"

"Fine. I'm okay. My case will come up before the end of the week. I know damn well it was a *good* shooting. I also know I was wrong not to call for backup."

Sophie rubbed Laura's shoulders in little circles. "Honey, why don't you do something to distract yourself?"

Laura twisted to look straight up at her mother. She thought, You mean like down a half pint of gin? She bit her tongue. "Ma, you're right. I'm going out. Maybe see a movie."

"Okay dear, will you be here for dinner?"

"Don't know, Ma. See you later."

Laura went upstairs and changed from her tee shirt and sweat pants into a trendy pair of tight black leather pants and a chartreuse pullover that flattered her perfect bosom and slender arms. She grabbed a roomy purse, packed a tooth brush and a change of silk and skimpy underwear, taking very little room. She checked her wallet. Plenty of cash. Fifties, tens and twenties. Money for greasing palms and loosening tongues. Feeling emboldened and more confident, she headed out.

Sophie frowned as she watched from the front room. "Laura?"

"See you later, Ma."

Getting behind the wheel of her MG was medicine to her. Driving helped her sort things out. The beginnings of a plan formed. The first order of the day. Locate Clyde. Finding a black man in an almost new white T-Bird shouldn't be too difficult.

The little MG ate up the road as she followed her usual route into NOLA. The trip was a soothing balm to her troubled soul.

Once arrived, she found a parking lot near the center and allowed the lot's attendant to tuck her tiny car away.

"This's a mighty fine ride, ma'am."

She smiled in spite of herself. Thought… hmmm, ma'am, not miss. "Yeah, thanks. Put her somewhere she won't get banged up," she said as she passed the long skinny almost grown man a twenty-dollar bill. "Yes, um. Gonna do jest dat. Thank you, ma'am. Thank you."

As providence would have it, Laura stopped to grab a quick bite and use the facilities and she overheard someone with a shaved head being discussed. Two fat brown-skinned women and one emaciated blonde girl sat together across the aisle. Three untouched classic club sandwiches, lettuce protruding from between toasted white bread, and three large colas waited. A whisper, loud enough to be deciphered. "Bianca ain't her real name is what I heard. I heard it was Mandy Rose."

Now Laura paused, reluctant to swallow the water in her mouth, lest she miss another clue.

The waitress bumped her hip against Laura's table; held up her order pad and pulled a pencil from behind her triple bejeweled ear. Laura yelped. "Coffee and a tuna sandwich on rye and that's all."

The waitress, thrown a curve 'cause she couldn't ask if that was all, scowled and scampered away. Did she mumble, "Rude?"

Laura tucked her hair behind her ears, craned her neck and eavesdropped.

"Yeah, that's where they took her."

"How do you know these things?"

"Just do."

Stick figure blondie piped up, "Why'd they take her?"

"Cause she had the juju."

Silence followed that bit of information. Laura licked her lips that'd gone dry. She knew what they were talking about. The juju was Clyde's damn gris-gris. "What to do. What to do."

She gave a little friendly wave to one of the corpulent ladies who responded with an icy cold stare.

Laura took a chance. Held up a twenty-dollar bill and crooked her finger in a c'mon over gesture. That did it.

The woman appeared to tell her seatmates, "Be right back." And made short work of closing the gap between their and Laura's table.

For such a large woman, she slid in the seat across from Laura with little effort. Laura put the twenty down and watched it get plucked and rolled and deposited in a blue denim shirt pocket.

"What's this for?"

"Anything you can tell me about where this Mandy Rose person was taken."

"Why do you care?"

"She's my sister."

"Oh, I understand. That woman sitting next to me is my sister. Familia esta muy importante."

Laura breathed a grateful sigh. "So, can you tell where she was taken?"

"I think so. The place is supposed to be secret, but everybody knows where it is and what it is."

Laura put a folded napkin in front of the woman and dropped a pen on it. "What's your name?"

"Tilly. What's yours?"

"Laura."

Tilly started to print the address, then added a helpful note. "Go armed."

Laura took another twenty out and squeezed it under Tilly's hand. Both women felt the exchange was of value.

Skinny blonde and dos chubby hermanas gawked but said nothing.

Laura was pleased she was in the general vicinity of her destination. The past year Laura'd become sensitive to the cumulative signs of an area disintegrating. Porches with broken stairs, shattered windows. Storefronts with iron bars were becoming common. A billboard atop a building with a peeling message encouraging the smoking of Marlboroughs. One cigarette from the pack stuck up, beckoning. And the smell. A mixture that always included urine.

Tilly had done good by her as she came to the address and recognized the building as it came into view. Laura patted her ankle, then on second thought, pulled her personal weapon, a tiny Beretta, out and tucked it into the small of her back. The tight leather pants were perfect camouflage.

She decided to be direct and boldly knocked on the mold infested door. *Tap, tap, tap.*

Nothing.

She banged the door. This time with the side of her fist. *Thump, thump, thump.*

The door slowly opened. A new smell. A mixture of male sweat and tobacco and something unnamable attacked her nostrils.

"Yeah, whaddya want lady?"

"I'm looking for someone."

"Yeah. Who?"

"A girl, really a young woman."

"Yeah. What for?"

"She ran away. I want to bring her home."

"Don't know no girl or no young woman. Go away." He started closing the door.

From inside Laura heard, "Who's that, Chalker?"

"Ah, someone looking for that broad we took." The one at "the place?"

Laura's eyes sparked.

The lummox noticed. He reached out to grab her, but she was too quick and too well-trained. She brought her knee up hard and fast into his unprotected testicles. He cried out and bent over to grab himself to cuddle his wounded anatomy. Laura stiffened the side of her hand and delivered an upper cut to his fat neck. He went down. On his knees now, she kicked him in the chin. Same voice as before, louder. "Chalker. What's goin' on?"

She didn't wait. She ran. Her amazing speed pleased her.

She knew she'd found where Mandy'd been taken. She'd heard "the place" alluded to, not only from Clyde, but also by street gossipers. Was she still there?

NOLA was full of secrets. Full of underground happenings. It was the home of jazz, beignets, Mardi Gras, gumbo and Voodoo. Secret rites and witches and bone gangs. And lots of SROs. Single Room Occupancies. Laura planned to get one. One within walking distance of Chalker and company. She arranged the bills in her wallet to hide the twenties and fifties. One sad light, still on the job of a tilted sign nailed to an overhead doorway spelled out one word. "Rooms." She was rethinking her choice of the black leather pants. She arranged her face with a down-turned mouth, pushed the back of her hair straight up and wiped her lipstick off. She had to look like a typical SRO customer.

Inside, the dark counter had two bony elbows leaning on it, a book with a torn cover sat between two knobby fingered hands. The owner lifted a stringy-haired head. The top crown smooth as a bowling ball. "Yes, miss. Watcha lookin' for?"

Laura kept it simple. "Need a room."

The clerk's eyes narrowed. The bowling ball leaned back to get a better gander at the woman in front of him. "This ain't too fancy."

"Just need a room."

"You a cop?"

Laura blanched. "Christ, no." Well, she thought, I am suspended.

"Awright lady." He shoved a three-ring binder to face her. "Sign your name. It's ten bucks a night. Cash only."

She picked up the ballpoint pen that felt greasy, being sure not to grimace and signed. "Mary Smith." Then got the money out.

He kept a straight face, observing the signature, snatched the ten-dollar bill so fast from her hand, she jumped.

He said, "Mary Smith, huh?" Then all on board, "Upstairs, first room on the right." He slid a key over to her.

"Thank you, sir."

Okay, now she had a base.

<h1 style="text-align:center">CHAPTER 30</h1>

Angus watched Sophie as she greeted him at the front door. She teetered on her straw-colored, open-toed wedgies. Her bloated face gleamed.

"Angus honey. Hi."

"Hi, where is everyone?"

They embraced for a few seconds. Sophie averted her face and held her breath. Too late. Angus smelled the alcohol coming out of her pores. "Everyone is everywhere. Nobody stays home anymore."

Cassy strolled into the great room and had a smile and pleasant hello for Angus. Angus said to Cassy, "Where's Laura?"

Cassy moved her jaw left to right, not happy about the answer. "I'm not sure. I think she went to find Mandy Rose. Also, Clyde."

Angus said under his breath, "Jesus." Out loud, he said, "She has to be there for her review. IA won't tolerate a no-show."

"She *knows* that Angus."

Sophie straightened up and chimed in, "Now Mandy Rose and Clyde and Laura are all missing." At that precise moment Hannah came in from her bedroom.

In a commanding voice she declared, "I'm hungry. Where's Almadine?"

Arriona, trailing behind her, answered, "Probably in the kitchen. Let's go get a snack."

Hannah said, "I'm not hungry for snacks. I want real food. Cooked food."

Angus wondered, not for the first time lately, why he got involved with all of this. He looked at Sophie, her blonde hair falling in golden ringlets to her shoulders. His heart melted. He'd ask Cassy to take her to some AA meetings again. Get her back on track. He said, "I'm hungry too. Let's see if we can eat early and watch television together later."

Hannah put one hand on her jutted hip, claiming victory.

Chapter 31

Laura freshened her bluish red lipstick and finger-combed her ash blonde bob. The mirror over the tiny sink in her rented room was brown around the edges and had a crack in the shape of the letter Y that was so ancient it was filled with dirt. Still, she looked good. Glad she'd worn comfortable shoes, she went down the stairs and out the door, ignoring the clerk, not wanting to start a hello and goodbye pattern. Once outside, the sun had settled, making dark shadows that crawled into alleys and around corners. Laura walked toward a building she remembered Clyde mentioning. He was secretive about his Voodoo underpinnings but let some names slip; usually when they'd been drinking all night. She was close to one he'd talked about. She intended to investigate it. Not positive it was the right place, she decided to take a chance. She remembered him talking about "the place." By the looks of it, she was on target.

The windows on the dirty brick building were covered. She stood by the front entrance; still as a cat about to pounce. She closed her eyes and listened. Took a few deep breaths and tuned in to "The Watcher."

"The Watcher" had been her close companion since early childhood. It was the force that observed from afar, had knowledge beyond her everyday cognizance. It saw all aspects of a situation; multiple perspectives. When engaged, Laura had an omniscient point of view. She never knew when it would activate, couldn't call it into action on command.

But right now, it screamed in her brain, "Knock on the door in front of you."

She obeyed. A firm full-knuckle rap. *Pow, pow, pow.* She waited for the door to be answered, raised her fist to follow with more knocks. Not necessary. The door creaked open. A nice-looking man with dark hair parted down the center, light colored eyes and full lips said, "Yes?" His voice was deep and creamy.

Laura went up on her toes to meet his eyes and queried, "I'm looking for my sister. I think she may be here."

"Your sister's name please."

"Mandy Rose, last name Bokum."

To her surprise, she got an answer. "Yes, she was here. Why do you want her?"

Laura thought, What a dumb ass. What she said was, "Because she's my sister. And because our family is worried about her."

"Come in, ma'am." He twisted his body to allow her passage. She smelled a sweet and spicy aftershave.

Laura was intrigued by the opulence inside. There were red velvet chairs with carved wood armrests and the floor was dark wood shined to a lustrous patina. A woman came through a passageway. Long rows of crystal beads fell from the arched opening, moving and making a pleasant crackling sound. The woman let the beads reassemble behind her.

Laura got a peek into the next room. It looked large and scantily furnished. There was the scent of smoke and the remaining smell of some kind of roasted meat that escaped through the beads. The woman had long black hair pulled to the front of her chest, tied with some kind of loose cork-like rope. Her eyes were slanted and heavily made up with dark purple eye shadow that continued under her eyes also. She wore a long purple robe with another length of cork-rope that encircled her waist. The two ends moved luxuriously as she floated in.

"She's looking for Mandy Rose, Ruby."

"I see. Why?"

"Says she's her sister."

"Oh. Won't you have a seat?" She gestured toward one of the burgundy chairs.

"No. Thank you. I'll stand. Is my sister here?"

"Yes, but there's been a problem."

Laura took a fast step closer. "What kind of a problem?"

"Does your sister suffer from a mental disorder?"

"Where's my sister?"

"I'm trying to help. Trying to tell you."

"Well, tell me."

"Your sister has had a nervous breakdown. We've had to seclude her for her own good."

"Where is she?"

"Please stay calm. She's okay, just has entered into a withdrawn state. A catatonic state. We're doing everything to help keep her safe."

"I don't understand. Why'd this happen? What'd you do to her?"

"We did nothing. She came to us already damaged. She was delving into things she had no experience with."

"What things?"

"As I'm sure you're aware, this is the home of Voodoo worshippers and neophytes from all walks of life. These seekers want more control over their lives. More power in their everyday lives."

Now Laura did sit down. The woman strode to her and placed a warm hand on Laura's shoulder. "Your sister is not a child. She is however, an infant in the ways of Voodooism."

Laura bristled. "What the hell do you mean?"

"She came here with a very powerful totem and no idea what it was capable of. She surrendered it easily to those who knew what it was. They are masters and priestesses."

"Can you take me to her?" Laura added, "please."

The woman snapped her fingers and turned her head quickly, almost insect like, toward the man who'd answered the door.

He went to Laura and lifted her arm, patted her hand. It was obvious she was to follow him. He led her past the hanging beads, into a large auditorium-size room, then through a doorway. Next they entered a short hallway with four closed doors. He stopped at the first one on the right; tapped lightly and entered. All very polite and proper seeming.

Laura's mouth gaped open as she saw Mandy Rose sitting on a rumpled bed on her haunches, rocking back and forth, back and forth. A young woman kneeled with her, making soothing cooing sounds as she rubbed Mandy's upper back.

"Mandy."

No response.

The man turned and left.

The young woman had a soft, almost musical voice. She studied Laura for a few seconds and announced, "You're Mandy Rose's sister, aren't you?"

"Yes, I am. What happened to her?"

"She's gone down under. It's her protective device. She wanted this. Wanted the experience. Wanted to leave the normal physical world behind." Pause. "Deeply hurt… your sister. She's been deeply hurt."

Laura's mind catapulted to the past. Jerked its way to dear old daddy and his prurient habits. He'd molested Mandy Rose for years. Laura's heart cried as though it'd been slashed. Daddy never bothered her; just Mandy Rose. Then he went on to abuse so many children that he'd helped kidnap. Once again, Laura felt pleasure that her father was knifed to death in prison. Good riddance to bad rubbish. Laura put her face near Mandy's and spoke her name in a whisper.

Mandy continued to stare at the blank wall, rocking to and fro and repeating the action. To and fro, nonstop.

"The Watcher" cupped Laura's face, an unusual occurrence, but it was what was needed.

It worked.

Laura knew she had to go easy, knew Mandy could be brought back. Mandy Rose was salvageable. Laura needed to find the key that opened her sister's bleeding heart and muddled mind.

A noise behind her made her look at the partially opened door. Heavy footsteps. Someone was coming.

CHAPTER 32

Hannah sat on her bed. As she looked around her room, she caught her reflection in the full-length mirror. Her face wavered like a heat-soaked mirage. It stilled; became frozen in time, grew younger. She stared transfixed by a version of herself long forgotten. But no; not forgotten, buried.

The Hannah in the mirror moved, turned to face her. She was at an odd angle, but the face was not. It glared at her full-frontal. So bright. The overhead light in the middle of the ceiling fan focused down on the face. The mouth's corners drooped down. Now tears appeared, great dollops of salt water running straight down both baby-fat cheeks. An indescribable urge came over her to hug the Hannah in the mirror. She wanted to wrap her arms around her five-year-old self.

She shook her head to lose the image, then looked back to see if the reflection had returned to a more normal duplication of what she should be seeing. Still there. Hannah turned her attention to her hands that were alive in her lap, wringing each other until her knuckles shone white from lack of blood. She gasped as her fingernails grew into talons; long and pointy. She held her hands out, palms down, in front of herself and observed normal pink shell-like little girl nails return.

"What's happening to me?"

She spoke out loud to the empty bedroom. Her voice had a lower quality. A timber unfamiliar to her ears. She listened, her body frozen and tight. Then her body expanded with warmth, erotic tremors, pleasure, danger and explosive power. The words were foreign.

"Ade due Damballa! Ade due Damballa! Ade due Damballa! Ade due Damballa!" The chant swirled around the room, increased with volume, then got softer and gentler but seemed to hold even more power.

Was there a scraping sound on her bedroom door?

Her tiny chest pumped up with a power-driven energy. She aimed

81

and pummeled the door with a blast of force that surpassed the physical wind and permeated the slab of wood. Surges of power blasted the door until it shook, hinges loosened until the pins wobbled, threatening to drop the door to the floor.

Hannah's face lost its contortions. A knowing smile graced a serene countenance.

CHAPTER 33

Sophie lifted her glass up high and eyed it. Empty already. She wasn't properly *removed* yet. Truth was she needed more and more to cope with all that was happening in her life. Mandy Rose still missing, and oh God, why did she cut all her hair off? *What does that mean?* And Hannah; little Hannah. She couldn't get close to that child. Her heart ached like an open bloody pit. The Hannah she remembered was sweet and loving. This new Hannah had a shell around her and even more disturbing; a meanness of spirit. The psychologists were trying to break through and find the horrible damage that'd invaded this little girl, old before her time.

Sophie jumped, dropped her empty glass as she identified where the strange thumping sound came from. Sounded like part of the house was under attack. A tornado? Arriona was staying late at school for a choral singing club. It must be Hannah.

Sophie let the glass stay where it lay on the orange mat. She slipped her sandals off and swallowed with a gulping sound. The lemon from her drink was tart in her mouth. Tiptoeing down the long hallway to the downstairs bedrooms took a minute; no more. The voice she heard was different. It had a sing-song quality. No, it sounded like someone was chanting. Who? Now she feared for Hannah. Was there an intruder in her bedroom. Was history repeating itself. Was someone going to snatch her again?

The words she heard became more identifiable. She'd heard Clyde making this same sort of chanting sounds. The words weren't English. They were foreign. They were confident and full of bravado.

She reached the bedroom door and stood in the hall, barely breathing. The door where she now knew her beloved granddaughter was making sounds that vacillated between guttural consonants and long drawn-out vowels. Sophie grabbed her own throat to squelch a possible dry cough. She wished she had her drink. Her heart pounded like a wild bongo drum. Her hands were cold and clammy as she resisted the almost painful urge to knock on Hannah's door.

Sophie decided to wait until Clyde was here to talk to him about this. Maybe it wasn't all bad. Maybe Clyde could make sense of it.

Hannah was in a trance. She was in love with the feeling of power that coursed through her very being, filled her body and her mind. She wanted more. She was hungry; no starved for her rightful station. She knew she was special.

Sophie made a small gasp when as the chanting tapered, she heard her granddaughter state, "I'm special."

CHAPTER 34

Laura's hand was steady. She reached for the pistol strapped to her ankle. It was a smart move.

"Don't try anything, sister. You ain't going nowhere. Nobody's gonna move a muscle." The two- hundred-pound brute lunged into the room with dangling ropes in his catcher's mitt paws. The meaty fingers were poised to find and secure feminine arms and legs. He reached for Laura, the most likely to put up a fight.

Not happening.

Laura would not let him take control. She slammed her hand to her ankle and with practiced expertise, whipped out her loaded weapon and fired.

The square-faced monster was beyond surprised. Shocked, his eyes turned into round amazed marbles, bugged out so far they threatened to tumble out of his head.

Laura did not want another dead body on her tab. But he needed to be stopped. She aimed for his chest. A second shot aimed next to the first brought the bully down so close to where Laura stood, his grasping hands touched her shins and splayed ropes flew to splat on the floor. A noteworthy abstract.

The rest of the coven had sent him to do a job; overestimated their scout's prowess, assumed he'd succeed in capturing yet another victim.

Laura took a look at the open-mouthed face of Mandy Rose's caretaker. She'd stopped rubbing Mandy and was bolt upright on her knees in a praying position, her hands clasped, fingers pointing toward heaven.

"Oh my God. You shot him."

"No time for that. Move. We gotta get out of here."

Camille didn't move a muscle. Laura slapped her hard across her face. *Crack.*

She said again, "Move."

Laura pulled Mandy off the bed by her shoulders. Mandy's mouth dropped in slow motion. Camille awakened to the dangerous situation and the need for fast action. She put her arm around Mandy Rose's waist and added her strength to Laura's. Laura needed one hand free for her pistol. She shot a quick glance at her firearm. Camille nodded and put her body under Mandy's to shoulder most of the weight. Luckily Mandy weighed less than a hundred pounds.

"Let's go."

The huge man on the floor groaned. Laura watched his eyes roll back in his head till only white shot through with red veins showed. She conjectured, maybe he won't die, no arteries clipped, judging by the amount of blood that oozed from his wounded legs.

The threesome moved past the unconscious lump and entered the hallway. Mandy's toes dragged across the floor, but they kept up aloft and were able to make headway. Once through the empty auditorium, they had to make it past the fancy front room.

The lone occupier sat at a gold ornate desk, one slender silken leg exposed from a slit in a long green dress, ending in a red stiletto high-heeled shoe. The noisy interruption made the woman twist. The red-high heel jerked. She gaped. "What the…"

Laura swung the pistol at her and gave it a threatening wave. The woman yelped. "Don't shoot."

Laura countered, "Don't move."

Mandy was using her legs now, making the exodus more manageable.

The woman at the desk reached for a phone. Too late. Laura caught the motion. A crack-shot, Laura had no problem pulverizing the phone. A splatter of blood; a smidgeon of collateral damage. That finger would never dial again or do much of anything else.

The rest of the escape was easy. The fresh night air was welcomed as Laura hailed a cab and debated on what to do with her sister and her sister's what? Roommate? Lover? Fellow prisoner? All three? Laura settled on all three. Directed the cabby to take them to the nearest hospital that had a psychiatric wing.

The cab driver raised his eyebrows till they disappeared under his blue cap. He put his elbow on the back of the passenger seat's headrest and took in the three women keeping a neutral expression except for the bushy eyebrows flight upward. "Well, took my wife's mother to Saint Francis Medical when she had her breakdown. Treated her real good, but she's still crazy as bat-shit."

Laura puffed out air, gave her head a quick shake and answered, "That'll do. No more conversation. Just take us there to the admittance entrance."

The cabby said, "Harrump." That spoke volumes. Then added, "Okay, missy."

Laura sat back, wondered where the hell Clyde was.

CHAPTER 35

"Sit your ass down and either come up with some answers or I'll throw your sorry ass in jail and forget about you."

The tall scrawny man licked his puffy lips. He had a red irritated ring under his lower lip where his tongue constantly overshot the target. It looked like a third lip. He burped and a loud growly noise escaped his innards as an encore. He was too scared to be embarrassed. He found his voice and croaked, "Detective Clark." Pause.

Angus waited, drummed his fingers on the long table in the interrogation room. His hard-boiled eyes drilled the man.

The man spoke. "I had nothing to do with hunting those kids, those little girls."

"So, you were in that building with those children as what? A benefactor?"

"Well, no, but I felt sorry for them."

"Is that supposed to give you a good citizen medal?"

"Well, no, but I wasn't gonna hurt them, wasn't gonna sell them neither."

Angus lurched forward, jutted his chin. "Sell them for what? Sell them to who? Who was gonna sell them?"

Skinny lip-licker slid lower in his metal chair. His tongue was working overtime. His hand came up to cover his chin. He spoke around his knuckles. "Those guys are bad. I only picked up the kids and brought them to that building."

"Why? What for?"

"The pay was good. I've got a wife and two kids of my own. I never asked any questions, just got the kids and delivered 'em."

Angus was losing patience. His face darkened. "What the hell did you think was gonna happen to those kids?"

Red lips sank lower. His stringy hair hung in ropey strands. "I didn't think. But now I see I was wrong. I'll tell you everything I know. I'll give you names. I'll give you numbers."

Angus slammed a pad in front of the subject, slapped a ball-point pen on top of the blank page. "Write."

He pushed himself up onto his elbows and knobby fingers picked up the pen. Angus watched as big printed letters started to appear on the sheet of paper. The man cocked his head to the right and squinted. That brought a fresh volley of big square words. First letters, then numbers.

Angus queried, "You want something to drink?"

The man looked up, eyes watery and nose drippy; said "Yes, please, water and a tissue too, please."

Angus Clark was satisfied. This had been productive. The list would go out immediately and on high priority. Kids came first with cops.

He left, listening to the sound of the pen scratching away to get a large cup of water and some tissues.

CHAPTER 36

Clyde kept swallowing. It was taking too long for the blood to stop. His head ached like a bulb-shaped toothache; front, back and center.

The big white sign said "Farmacia" in black letters. He stumbled through the door. It had information in Spanish on it. He needed help. He had to get his tongue to stop bleeding.

The pharmacist took one look at the handsome Black man who had fresh blood trickling from the side of his mouth. Compassion ruled. He waved to Clyde and locked into his gaze. He opened and closed his fingers to beckon Clyde to come to him. The pharmacist sat high on a perch that overlooked the entire drug store.

Desperate now, Clyde obeyed.

"How did this happen to you, sir? Should I call the polizia?"

Clyde's swollen tongue dripped blood. Talking was labored. "No thur. Pleath, no copths."

"Okay, no cops. Can you let me see inside your mouth?"

Clyde was happy for the help and felt less prejudice from the Latino than he would've felt from a white guy. The pharmacist left his medical balcony and walked around to where Clyde stood. "Hi, my name's Rodolpho, what's yours?"

"Itth's Clyde."

"Okay Clyde, can you open your mouth for me?"

"Yeth."

Clyde opened as wide as he could. He was becoming more and more alarmed at the unceasing red river that poured from his injured tongue.

"Ah, I see what's going on. Your tongue, as you know, has been lacerated. It's quite deep and requires a doctor's care. Some cuts like this can heal on their own. Not this one, I'm afraid." He took Clyde's elbow and led him to a wooden chair that had a sign over it that read "De Espera."

90

The leather seat felt soothing to Clyde's buttocks that was also bruised on the edges. Embarrassed, he blinked back tears.

With a short walk down an aisle, the good man plucked a red and white box from a shelf, opened it, and returned to Clyde. He unrolled some surgical pads and using the tips of his fingers, he extracted several and handed them to Clyde. Without instruction, Clyde knew to put them on his tortured tongue to stem the unremitting flow of blood.

"I'm calling a cab to take you to the emergency room. You'll likely need stitches."

Clyde nodded at his copper-skinned benefactor. He was overwhelmed by such kind attendance. He felt sleepy and let his head drop to his shoulder, keeping his hand on his poor mouth so the gauze stayed inside, blocking the grisly flood.

Several minutes passed and the pharmacist tapped his shoulder. "Your cab's here."

Clyde pressed some cash into the pharmacist's white coat pocket as he entered the cab.

The cabby looked none-too-happy. He frowned. A bleeding Black man could spell trouble.

Not intimidated, the pharmacist gave the hospital's address and threw Clyde's wad of bills onto the empty front passenger seat. "That'll more than cover it. Thank you."

The cabbie touched his pudgy fingers to the brim of his cap and put the vehicle in gear.

Less than ten minutes later, the taxi pulled into the hospital's emergency room. The driver stated crisply, "Here's where you get out."

Clyde awakened from a twilight sleep as the vehicle lurched to a stop. He looked up at the well-lit entrance from the cab's dark interior and squinted. Red and white lights made the windows of the cab a circus of color.

The cab driver reached back and poked Clyde on the shoulder, hard. "You get out now."

Clyde got the message. He shut the door, which didn't quite catch, and looked toward the big glass doors of the ER entrance. The taxi roared off; the inside lights blazing courtesy of the unlatched door.

Clyde tried to figure out if he should go through the massive glass doors or find a one-person doorway. He never had to decide. Someone appeared in a green outfit and put an arm around his back and steered him into the hospital. Noise and chaos greeted him. He let his hand drop from monitoring the bloody gauze, which followed and plopped down by his feet. A gurney was headed his way; another green outfit. He recalled that people bleeding or people with anaphylactic reactions were taken and treated first.

A howl broke into his machinations. A familiar howl.

Ignoring the new red purge, he followed the sound of the wail to a trio of excited female voices who entered to his right. They were at an "Admittance" sign and appeared to be giving information.

One of the three was on a gurney; not wanting to stay there. The unhappy rider was twisting its body in a bid for freedom. Two hospital workers were holding the person in place as two other workers were barreling toward the melee with long white straps that trailed behind them. The human being on the gurney took an almost athletic and cunning whirl that allowed Clyde a view of the unhappy person's face. The cropped hair stood straight up like grass growing on a skull. Something familiar. Yes, oh my God… yes. He almost passed out. His knees buckled. His brain put out a silent scream. *Mandy.*

He was caught by his caretakers under his armpits and thought to be in danger of bleeding out. They acted fast; lifted him as though he was a feather pillow, applied clean gauze and pressure to his tongue, leaving him unable to utter a word or cry out to Mandy Rose. Soon a dark velvety gray claimed him. He welcomed it.

He'd find Mandy Rose later. Yes, he'd find his daughter's mother.

CHAPTER 37

Detective Angus Clark was still not home from the precinct. The mansion was in subdued lighting and both Hannah and Arriona were asleep in their beds.

Cassy stroked Sophie's forehead while the older woman made muffled noises, attempting to quieten the crying.

"I'm worthless. I was a lousy mother and now I'm a lousy grandmother. I just want it all to stop. I want to die." The stench of alcohol was overpowering. The previous bout of vomiting had done nothing to purge the cloying odor. Sophie continued her litany of self-pitying misery. "Angus is sick of me and I don't blame him. I'm fat as a buffalo again and don't make him happy. He should leave me."

"C'mon Sophie, go put a clean dress on and change those soaked slippers for shoes. Almadine is here for the girls. We need to get you to a meeting."

Sophie glowered. "What for? AA doesn't work for me."

"Let's go anyway. Change your clothes. We can still make most of the meeting."

"I don't know, Cass. That meeting is no good. They've seen me before. I'll look like a loser going back there again."

Cassy retorted, "We're not going to your usual meeting. We're going to one I know about. Guaranteed no one there'll know you."

Sophie mopped tears and mucus from her face with the yellow lace hanky she held in a boxer's grip. Cassy gently pried the limp material from Sophie's hand and replaced it with a doubled-up tissue. "C'mon, clean up and let's go." Cassy inspected the drooping curls on Sophie's shoulders and swiped at them with a clean tissue till the damp tendrils were free of regurgitated particles. She also rubbed the yoke on her dress with the same caring attention. "Never mind changing. Just put on some shoes and let's go."

Sophie raised murky blue eyes to Cassy's deep chocolate ones and nodded.

Almadine entered. She took in the drama taking place. Always perceptive, she said, "You gals go on. I'm staying right here to take care of everything and everyone."

The two women emerged, arm in arm. Cassy said partly to herself, "Forget about the damn slippers. Nobody will even notice or care."

Cassandra opened the door to Sophie's Jag and helped lower Sophie into the passenger seat. Cassy knew where she was headed. The upscale neighborhood slid away under the wheels of the pricey silver vehicle. The streets became narrower and darker. Cassy arrived at her destination. There were sounds of a soft wheezy snoring slipping from a now peaceful looking Sophie whose mouth hung open, shiny with a bit of drool.

The church lot was jammed with over ten-year-old vehicles. The building had a bright, almost blue light over the doorway, which was closed. Sophie's messy blonde head popped up when the car lurched to a stop. "Huh? Where are we, Cass?"

"AA meeting."

"Where did you take me?"

"To a different meeting. New for you, but not to me. I came here a lot of years ago with a friend. She never got the program and died drunk. I had to ID her body. That's not gonna happen to you."

"Yeah, but Cass."

"No yeah buts. Let's go inside."

The short nap had been beneficial. Sophie'd stopped crying. She did as she was told. There was a musty basement odor as they single-filed down the narrow staircase. Inside, a few heads turned as they entered. It was a well-attended meeting. A table against a side wall held neat stacks of AA pamphlets and a stainless steel coffee urn looked ready to give up the universal drink for attendees. Two open boxes of donuts were on display as well as paper cups, etc.

Sophie's eyes ballooned like giant blue marbles. She gazed from the goodie table to the participants around the long table and clasped her mouth and balked. Cassy knuckled the small of her back to keep her moving.

As providence would have it, there were two empty metal chairs next to each other. They tiptoed over and scraped them out as quietly as possible; sat and tucked their knees under the table.

Wide awake, Sophie felt mostly sober. There was one other white face in the room. The facilitator, a large Black man with heavy eyelids and a warm toothy smile, announced, "We'll take a ten-minute break now. Help yourselves to coffee and donuts, courtesy of our goody volunteers for tonight's meeting."

There was an immediate rumble of sliding chairs and exodus to the coffee and sweets table. Sophie wanted coffee. Cassy surmised as much and joined the group taking turns with the spigot.

"Why don't *she* get 'er own coffee, lady?"

Cassy jerked her head around to face a tall skinny Black woman dressed all in green. The response was quick and calculated to ease the tension that was building. "We take turns getting each other coffee."

Green dress squinted at this peaceful explanation. Several others watched the interaction. Another woman placed her hand on a green sleeve and said, "C'mon Stella, be nice."

Stella wasn't convinced and challenged loudly, "Who are you? You ain't never been here before."

Cassy kept her voice low and neutral. "I'm Cassy. What's your name?"

"Never you mind my name. What's *her* name?" She shot a glance to where Sophie sat looking pale and stricken.

A large droopy lidded man sidled over to the fray, sporting a yellow-stained toothy smile. "What's going on there, Stella?"

"I don't like her looks."

"Well, we can't always like everyone, but we try to keep an open mind and accept them in here."

Stella clamped her lips together into a thin pencil line; still looking pissed.

Cassy brought a well-sugared coffee along with her own creamy brew to Sophie, and they sat and sipped.

The meeting resumed. Everyone seemed rejuvenated from the caffeine and sugar fix.

"Let's continue. For any newcomers; you may listen or contribute as you choose. Stay after the meeting if you want to talk. Tonight's meeting is on the slogans."

A short pause and baggy lids looked toward the next person; a middle-aged woman who wore her graying hair sleeked and straight back in a bob. "My name is Millie. I'm an alcoholic."

Murmers of, "Hi Millie."

"I've been coming here to these rooms for a lot of twenty-four hours. I'm never gonna stop 'cause I'm never gonna graduate. I use the slogans. I use 'how important is it?' all the time. I used to make mountains out of molehills; get caught up in a trap of my own making. Everything was a huge problem. Even picking out peanut butter at the grocery store. Decisions would paralyze me. Then I started getting things in order. I love the slogans, but right now, that's my favorite. That's all I have to say."

"Thank you for sharing, Millie."

Next to Millie was a young attractive woman, maybe even still a teenager. She wore large round glasses that accented beautifully made-up eyes. Lavender eye shadow and black eye-lining top and bottom, thick lashes that must've been store-bought. The effect was astonishing.

"Hi, my name's Chelsea and I'm an alcoholic. I'm also a drug addict and attend NA; narcotics anonymous." Pause. "I love the slogan, "One day at a time," always have to repeat to myself… poor me, poor me, pour me another. I ain't been sober or clean for that long, so a tall glass of amber liquid still looks might good to me."

A few chuckles of understanding passed through the group.

"Yep, it sure does. The part that's hard for me is the self-pity. The poor me stuff."

Sophie blinked. She was really listening now.

The young girl continued. "Yeah, I know self-pity and resentments are deadly for an alcoholic."

Sophie thought of Harry.

"If I let myself, I can get on the pity pot until I think I deserve that drink. After all I've been through, all the suffering. Yeah, poor me. But I'll keep coming, and I'll call my sponsor when I feel myself slipping." The woman closed and opened those magnificent eyes and stopped speaking.

Sophie felt her face go dry and taut. Cassy sensed the energy.

The next to talk was a neatly dressed older Black man in a worn but crisp brown suit. He looked over seventy. He wore rimless glasses and was frail almost to the point of emaciation. He also wore a pleasant smile. "My name is Sam; I'm an alcoholic; a grateful alcoholic. I'm kind of a fixture around here. Some say an old-timer. Love this meeting. My slogan tonight is "God don't make junk." Some here know my story, some might need to hear it. My daughter's daughter, my beautiful granddaughter died a homeless person. She never could get sober. Some don't make it. Recovery and sobriety have to come from within. She had friends in this program who tried to help." His gaze went directly to Cassandra. Sophie thought she saw big fat droplets erupting from Cassie's big brown eyes. She looked more closely at her friend's face, a questioning stare on her own. Cassy nodded. Sophie put her hand on her friend's forearm. The tears were cascading down shiny chocolate cheeks.

Why does it take us so long to know the pain in the hearts of others?

Sophie renewed her resolve to get sober. This time she would do it. One day at a time.

She patted Cassy's arm and sat up straighter in her metal chair.

CHAPTER 38

Laura stayed behind at admittance. Camille kept her fingertips on the back of Mandy Rose's shored head. She couldn't see her arms, which were now encased in what is commonly called a straitjacket. Mandy had gone quiet again. Her nodding head with its cropped hair resembled a maniacal Bobblehead doll. Her chin scraped left and right on her chest. She felt no pain. The coarse material of the medieval encumbrance showed a bloody swath in a ruddy arc.

Laura was insistent on seeing where Mandy was going to be taken, but the intake nurse was full of self-importance and resisting cooperation. "The information must be accurate, Ms. Bokum. What is your exact relationship to this young woman?"

Laura, who never suffered fools gladly, gave a laconic response. "Sister."

The nurse's eyebrow went up, just one. "Who was that with your…" hesitation, "…sister?"

"I can't answer that. I don't know."

"Excuse me. Please explain. You came in with both of them, and you say one is your sister and the other, you don't know?"

Laura lost it. "Just met her. Don't know her."

Clyde put his hand on the rubberized wheel of the wheel chair he sat in and stopped it cold. The orderly yelped an "Oomph" as his stomach took the brunt of the abrupt halt. Still bleeding, Clyde managed a strange sounding yell. "Gaura"

Laura pivoted; her pissed off wrinkled brow deepened. She jumped high as she spotted the wheelchair debacle and the familiar passenger. She left the pompous intake person, mouth agape and pencil poised, to wonder what had interrupted her very important information gathering mission.

Laura was by Clyde's side in less than ten seconds. She gasped at all the blood on his face, hands and shirt. He said, "Itʰ's nothing, bit my thungue." Then his eyes widened. "Gandy?"

"Oh Clyde, we have a lot to talk about. Mandy is being admitted. She's finally had a total mental breakdown."

Clyde shook his head, both eyes turned down on the edges.

The orderly in charge of the wheelchair, while very patient, needed to get his still bleeding patient to the waiting room to be seen by the intern on call. "Might I suggest miss, that you finish checking in the woman you brought here; then go down the hall to room number three to continue this discussion with this patient."

Laura agreed. "I'll be right there, Clyde. Then I'll find out where they're taking Mandy Rose."

Clyde was pleased he could articulate the word "Good" without sounding drunk. He marveled at the chances of him, Laura and Mandy being in the emergency room at the exact same time.

Was his gris-gris at work?

CHAPTER 39

It was on the fourth floor. Only close family could be admitted.

Clyde was getting a dissolving suture to close the gap in his tongue.

Mandy Rose had gone morgue quiet; her throat raw from her screaming episode.

The elevator rumbled upward. The two women eyed each other; thrown together in an escalating crisis that was family oriented. Or was it?

"So, are you older or younger than Mandy Rose, or do you call her Bianca?"

Laura bit her healthy tongue and looked at the ceiling in the elevator. "Bianca?"

"Yes, sorry. Of course, that's not your sister's real name. Right?"

Laura took a needed breath and answered, "Don't know anything about the name Bianca. Yes, Mandy is fine, and I'm younger."

"Oh, and Clyde?" Camille was pushing the envelope here. Wanted to find out whatever she could.

"Wait a minute. I should be asking you the questions. What were you doing in that room in that horrible place? And why was my sister there?"

It was Camille's turn to take a deep breath. She understood Mandy's sister was stressed and opted to keep emotions at a low level. "Yes, of course you'd want to know all that. I can't pretend to have all the answers. Is it Laura or Lorie?"

"Laura." Impressed with the calm demeaner of Mandy's roommate, Laura was nevertheless hungry for facts. She waited for more.

"Okay, Laura. I'm not sure I would've been able to escape if you hadn't shown up. Mandy was in the same predicament. It has to do with the energy inherent in some amulets. Ones that are eons more powerful than the run of the mill ones; some of these lesser amulets have little to no capabilities. The dynamic force of the gris-gris the greedy corrupt criminals took from your sister is beyond any other jujus known or possibly as yet undiscovered. This goes back to its origins in Africa, and it's believed to hold monumental power for evil or for good luck. African slaves brought in from Senegal and Mali in the seventeenth and eighteenth centuries brought in some of these artifacts installed in their bodily orifices. I overheard discussion that a small percentage of these gris-gris are inscribed with scriptures that tell a story of unmitigated power." Camille had a faraway look on her face as she shared these facts.

The elevator had come to a full stop. Camille pressed the *close* button three times. They stood in a kind of limbo. A surge of energy circulated in the small box car. Laura felt tingly and knew "The Watcher" was on high alert.

Camille tilted her head back and pointed her finger at Laura. "What's going on, Laura?"

"I have contact with an energy source that has served as a guide throughout my life. It's picking up on your diatribe."

"Okay. Let's get off and find a seat in the hall. I'll finish explaining. We have some time before they'll let us in to see Mandy."

They found a wooden bench and settled onto it next to each other. Laura said, looking directly into the eyes of Camille only two inches away, "And, so?"

Camille stretched her jaw and continued. "The collective wants to gather any power that has been conveyed to anyone who's had the totem in their possession. And, more importantly, they want to get the rightful heir. This would be your sister's daughter. The daughter of Clyde Boudreaux. The girl's name is Hannah."

Laura's hand flew to her mouth. "Do they know where to find Hannah?"

They would've gotten that from Mandy or from Clyde if they had them in their clutches. It's called "Harvesting."

Laura's hand absently pawed at her own cheek. "And why were you there with her?"

"Much the same reason. However, the Boudreaux's gris-gris is," she paused, a mixture of fear and awe clouding her features, "I cannot stress this enough, is more forceful than any other and would bestow great and intense power on its rightful owner. This is always a priestess. A female. This would be Hannah."

Laura's blood went cold. Though the hospital's corridor was rather hot and stuffy, she shivered and rubbed her upper arms. "The Watcher" gave credence to this repartee, telling Laura it was accurate. It was truth.

A double door flung open and a tall Asian man with dull black hair and thick rectangular glasses approached. His face was a concerned question mark. He touched his chin for half a second and several long strides put him in front of Laura and Camille who'd stood up rapidly, maybe too fast. Camille felt a bit light-headed, maybe low blood-pressure, however she recovered in a few instants.

"Are you related to the young woman we just admitted to the psyche unit?" He had remnants of an accent.

"Yes, I'm her sister. How is she?"

"Well, I'm afraid right now she's not communicating at all. It's what is called a state of catatonia. It can last a few hours or days or persist for much longer periods of time. Basically she has retreated from reality. We'll do all we can to bring her around. First, we'll administer neuroleptics and if that produces no improvement, we'll consider ECT, better known as Electro-shock therapy. That has had good results in many cases."

Laura stood, saying nothing yet. Camille put her arm around her. "When can I see my sister?"

"She's completely sedated now. I suggest returning in the morning. We can discuss further treatment then and may know more."

Just then the elevator door noisily opened and Clyde burst out; wild eyed. The doctor's face tightened. "Who…"

Laura explained before more could be said. "This is my sister's husband."

Camille's eyes brightened as she ogled the now, cleaned of all blood, handsome man.

The doctor rearranged his features and nodded a greeting to the newcomer. He felt it prudent to say again, "Tomorrow morning you may visit Miss or uh Missus Mandy Rose." Did he get that right? He thought for the third time that day, "I need a vacation."

Clyde went right up to Laura and flung his arms around her. The doctor did a tiny head shake, then moved on down the hallway where he likely had an office where he could digest all of this. Maybe have a shot of Bourbon.

A good night's sleep would help. *Tomorrow morning will be here soon.*

<h1 style="text-align:center">CHAPTER 40</h1>

The group of girls in the school courtyard bunched together, like one entity. A hive with a discernable buzzing sound emanating from the batch of pre-puberty females. Skinny legs and pointy elbows prevailed. There was a nucleus. A submergence in the clan. A power center?

Arriona observed, leaning into a copper-colored fence at the edge of the yard, her best friend stuck to her side, also leaned. Melly was loyal and almost as smart as Arriona. Her light brown skin shone in contrast to Arriona's rich chocolate coloring.

"What's she like to live with?"

"Mel, it's more like I live with her and she doesn't let me forget it."

Melly pushed her tongue into her cheek in thoughtfulness. "I know you told me she was kidnapped, so maybe that's why she's so weird?"

"Uh no, it's more than that. I can't explain it. It's like she's a kid, but not a kid; like she's a grown woman." Pause. "No, that's not right either. Sometimes she sings songs using words I don't understand. And once…" she paused again, "…maybe I shouldn't tell you this."

"Arry, you can tell me anything. It'll be secret. Nobody could beat it out of me."

Arriona sighed; a deep sigh that lasted until her chest had dropped and her shoulders slumped. She looked over at the clump of girls and twisted her bottom lip to aid the decision-making process. Her eyes went to mid-distance and she started again. "Once I found something in her clothes closet. I was looking for my huarache sandals that I missed. I couldn't find them for weeks." Arriona swallowed. "I saw a piece of straw on the floor. It was the same brownish color as my sandals. I got on my knees and reached in to investigate." Arriona stopped speaking.

Now Melly was wide-eyed, holding her chin with her palm, wanting her friend to continue. Still, Arriona remained silent.

"Arry, what was it? Was it your shoes?"

Arriona blinked a few times and became animated. Her brows furrowed and she took up the halted dialogue. "It was a doll. A rag doll. I slipped my hand under it to get a better look. It was not a regular rag doll. It was tied together with strands from my sandals. The body was no color, just a dirty white and stuffed. But the face, oh my God Melly, the face." Another pause. "The mouth was stitches; a mouth sewn shut. And the eyes were like black holes. It stared at me with those hideous black smudges." Arriona was reliving the horror.

Melly whispered, "What did you do?"

"I dropped it. It made a heavy clunk sound. No rag doll would ever do that."

An eerie chorus rose from the bevy of school girls. Arriona and Melly watched and listened. It sounded like chanting. Like the chanting from a current movie they'd seen about a witch's coven. The words were different. There were only two words being mouthed. Over and over, the same two words.

"Hail Hannah. Hail Hannah. Hail Hannah."

CHAPTER 41

Angus had endured the angry diatribe from Captain Richard Sloane. Rick's blue eyes stood out like traffic lights in an inflamed ruby colored face. Angus felt his blood pressure rising in response.

Angus sat at his desk now, his office door closed. He replayed some of the phrases from the rant; the tirade still ringing in his ears. It was more than a scolding. It was a shredding. The worst part Angus ruminated was that the captain was right. Damn right. He never should've sent Laura and Cassy out to interview CIs. It was against the rules. Protocol breached. To make it worse, it had gone south in the extreme. Laura had killed a man. Self-defense the likely conclusion, but they shouldn't've been out there. Too early. Too green.

He shuffled the papers on his desk and reread the report on the takedown house. Tilting his head, he bargained with his conscience. *Progress is being made. We rescued those kids. They were not with those monsters long enough to be hurt too badly. Not long enough for permanent damage.* This took his mind to young Hannah.

What had happened to that little girl? What had those captors done to her? He cringed. He thought of Sophie. His poor sweet Sophie. How she'd suffered. He wanted to make her happy. Make her life better. He dropped his head into his hands and noted with unpleasant alarm that his nose dripped onto the pile of paper he'd wrinkled with his elbows. No, some of those drops were from his eyes. He shot a look at his door to confirm it was locked. It was.

The names marched across his mind. Sophie, Laura, Hannah, Mandy Rose. Even Clyde. He couldn't fix any of them. He remembered his dear mother. Dear Pearl. He'd watched her die. Couldn't fix her.

This must be what poets called the dark night of the soul.

105

CHAPTER 42

A lone squad car pulled up to a brick building, seldom approached by police or for that matter, civilians living near the cloistered structure.

Twenty minutes ago the 911 caller said, "I heard what sounded like gunshots coming from that crazy place where they kill goats and do Voodoo."

"What's your name, ma'am?"

"Never mind that."

"Did you see anything?"

"Yeah, saw three guys leave by the front door."

"Can you describe these men?"

"Wasn't men, was ladies." *Bang*! Dial tone.

The emergency call dispatcher jerked her head back and rubbed her ear. She never knew when to expect the slam of the receiver in these calls.

The two officers in the squad car looked at the building, noting the slightly open front door. "Should we call for backup?"

"I dunnoh. The two of us should be okay. Let's go in."

One tall skinny officer with a blond crew cut and harelip emerged from the passenger side, pistol drawn. The driver joined him; a Black man with close cropped matte black hair, high-waisted with long legs, hand on his revolver that was partially out. They approached cautiously but boldly. Both dropped into a crouched position.

A high-pitched wailing erupted from within. "Sounds like someone's hurt." They broke into a trot.

The room was lavish. The woman slumped half on the floor and half in a chair that looked like it belonged in a museum. Her fingers dripped blood, bright ruby drops that coated her hand and traveled up her bent arm as she held it up. The Black officer went to her. He took out his Rover and called for an ambulance. The other officer kept his pistol out and waved it, shouting, "Anyone here?"

106

No answer.

The first officer helped the stricken woman disengage her leg from the chair and slipped her down to the floor. He put her gushing, now three-fingered hand on top of her stomach. He felt nauseous at the sight of the green ring still in place at the base of her pinkie

Again, the shout, "Anyone here? Police." Gun leading the way, he traveled to a room on the right of a hallway, door ajar. He kicked the door open and went in sideways. He faced a strange scenario. A bed with dishes on it; bones in a bowl, lined up as though making a statement. A Sunday barbecue? "What the hell?"

A large man sprawled on the floor; not moving. He stared at the ceiling. Both eyes were clouded. The strong odor of released bowels gave little doubt. This man was dead. Two small round bloody holes. Straight through his barrel-shaped chest. He was still warm.

Who else had been in this room? Did that person or persons murder this man? Not men, but women apparently. Or were there men that'd left earlier? And did these same perps shoot the fingers off the fallen woman by the desk? What had gone on here?

A crackling sound announced his Rover phone reporting a response from headquarters. He answered, "Officer Daniels here. We have a wounded person and a dead body. Requesting an ME or coroner asap and additional personnel for this crime scene. I already called for a bus for the wounded woman; on its way." Daniels listened, "Yes, that's where we are." Another pause. He said, "Didn't see any dead goats, assuming you're serious. Did see some bones on dinner dishes. All I'm saying right now that I can confirm."

Screaming from the front room. The woman's face grotesquely distorted, sweaty and red. "Calm down, ma'am. You'll be fine. Ambulance is on its way."

"I won't be fine, look at my God damn hand. My fingers are blown off. That bitch shot me. I know what she looks like."

The cop studied the pitiful pulp where the lady's fingers used to be. His belly made a strange burping sound. He flattened his hand over his stomach, smoothing it in an attempt to calm the storm brewing in there. "Let's get you to the hospital first. I'll personally meet you there and as soon as you're treated for your injuries, you can give your statement and description of the shooter."

"Oh, I'll describe her all right. That woman is a murderer. I heard her shoot Clem. Is he okay? Is he dead? She's dangerous. A killer."

"Please try to relax. The ambulance is here."

Two young men entered with a stretcher and portable oxygen. Both handsome Latinos. They worked together to hoist the furious woman onto the gurney and attempted to put the oxygen mask over her nose and mouth. She was having none of that, slapping away with her uninjured hand.

She bellowed, "She's a murderer. I want her arrested. She's a killer." After batting away the oxygen mask, she exhaled and seemed a trifle spent.

As she was taxied out the open door, she twisted her head back and managed one more time, "She's a murderer."

One of the handsome young men finally got her to accept the oxygen mask.

She settled down.

CHAPTER 43

The over six-foot tall swarthy doctor looked striking in his white physician's jacket. His stethoscope swung easily as he took long strides into the waiting cubicle where Laura and Camille were watching over Mandy Rose, who still just sat and stared. Unable, without her help, to get her onto the patient table, they'd trundled her into the visitor's chair. Mandy's head hung low.

"Who is responsible for this young woman?" The doctor took stock of Mandy's posture and lack of facial expression, already aware of the catatonia diagnosis.

Laura spoke up. "I am. I'm her sister."

"What is your name, please?"

"Laura Bokum and my sister is Mandy Rose Bokum."

The doctor's dark brows knotted as he stooped low to peer directly into Mandy's face. "How long has she been like this?"

With a twist of her head and raised brows, Laura consulted Camille.

"About two or three hours."

"Do either of you know if she's taken any drugs?"

Camille wondered if any had been administered to her during the "ceremony." "I'm not sure; not that I saw her take."

"What does that mean?"

Camille took in a deep breath and exhaled as she dealt with fears of possible consequences of being discovered giving information on the Voodoo practices the thugs used to keep people in line. She had mixed emotions. She rather liked Mandy Rose.

The doctor tried again. "What do you mean? Are you saying someone might've drugged her against her will?"

Camille faltered. "Um, maybe. I don't know."

"May I have your name to please."

"Camille."

"Last name?"

"Turner," Camille lied.

"Tell me what you know of what happened to this young woman."

Camille described the Voodoo ceremony, the imbibing of the roasted goat. She added that Mandy had seemed okay through all of that.

The doctor was a patient man, but he was picking up on a reluctance to continue the story from Camille Turner. He waited almost a full minute then turned to Laura. "Were you there during any of this?"

Laura tensed her spine and held her palm up to Camille whose open mouth had happily clamped shut. She wanted out of there.

"Doctor, when I got to the room where they were staying, my sister was sitting on a makeshift bed, rocking back and forth and staring straight ahead as though seeing nothing."

"And then what?"

"I wanted to get them out of that place."

"What place?"

"Camille can give you the exact address, but it seems to be an underground headquarters for occult Voodoo practices."

"Okay, this is helpful. Please continue."

"I was concerned; focused on my sister, so I was shocked when a huge man violently burst into the room. His eyes were wild, and he threatened us. He had ropes in his massive hands. He grinned and charged at me." Laura paused.

The doctor jutted his head; encouraged her to continue.

"I was armed. I pulled out my revolver and shot him. I had to stop him."

"Your revolver?" The doctor's eyes went round. Two glistening shot glasses.

"Yes, the gun was strapped to my ankle."

"Have the police been called?"

"I am the police."

"What the…"

"Yes, I am the police. I'm temporarily under suspension."

"For what?"

"I shot and killed a man."

The good doctor grabbed the edge of the nearby shelf, his stethoscope hanging in mid-air.

Camille watched Laura with hero-worshipping eyes.

Mandy Rose sat, slumped over and staring.

The doctor recovered, brought himself erect again, cleared his throat and said, "And then what? Did you all leave and taxi here?"

"Well, no."

"No?"

Laura continued. "No, then we headed for the door holding Mandy Rose up between us. She needed help. There was a woman in the front room, seated at a desk. She went for her phone. I was pretty sure of the kind of friends she'd be dialing. I stopped her from making that call."

How did you stop her?"

"I shot her."

The doctor's cocoa-colored face morphed into a grayish white moon stone, even his lips lost color. "You shot her?"

Laura explained, "Just the phone and her fingers got involved somehow."

"I see." The normally shock-proof doctor leaned into the wall as the blood and oxygen returned to his features. "Have the police…" he paused "…other than you, been informed?"

Camille felt obliged to weigh in. "We were gonna get Mandy Rose taken care of first. We also felt the gunshots would probably have alarmed neighbors and they'd call the cops."

"All right, Camille. Please go and do that now. There's a phone out this door and to the left. Punch in 000 to get an open line. And Camille, maybe you shouldn't leave yet."

Camille hurried from the room.

"Please check on my sister, Doctor."

The tall man's face had returned to normal as he took a small pen light out of his white coat pocket. He crouched to align himself with the motionless girl. He passed the little beam back and forth in front of her unfocused pale blue eyes; barely a flicker. "I'm going to admit her."

"Yes, that's good. Thank you, Doctor."

"First, I'll take a blood sample to rule out any drugs."

"You have a psychiatric ward here, right?"

"Yes, a very good one too."

Laura nodded.

"It's not my job to detain you, but it's better for you if you turn yourself in, Laura."

"I know. I will."

Laura bent over her older sister and hugged her with both arms. Then she kissed the top of her prickly haired head and left.

Camille was nowhere to be seen. Laura ignored the public phone and jogged in a sprint, finger already aimed at the elevator button that would speed her descent out of the hospital and back into the bowels of NOLA. She intended to uncover the loathsome, evil acts being committed under the guise of the Voodoo creed, in the name of religion.

The night was still warm from the day's sweltering heat, but the muggy air felt rejuvenating as her thirsty face loosened under the generous New Orleans moisture.

The caterwauling of a police siren jacked her blood pressure as she walked briskly, taking a fast corner up a side street. She patted her gun, rolled her sleeves up over her shoulders and unfurled the black kerchief she carried, which became a do-rag, hiding any trace of her ash blonde hair.

She'd learned in the police academy how to disguise herself in record time from the miscreants who wrote the book.

The mission had begun.

CHAPTER 44

"Bokum residence. Almadine speaking. Can I help you?"

The low-pitched voice sounded calm and official. "I'd like to speak with any relative of a Laura Bokum, please."

The serious tone of the caller chilled Almadine, made her chin quiver, but didn't throw her off her unflappable nature. "That would be Mrs. Sophie Clark, Laura's mother. I'll get her for you. Please hold on."

Sophie was in the kitchen reaching into the refrigerator for the pitcher of lemonade; a tall glass already full of ice cubes in her free hand. "Mrs. Bokum, um, I mean Clark, um, I mean Sophie, there's a man on the phone who wants to speak to you. It's about Laura."

"About Laura?" The glass crashed to the tile floor sending ice cubes scattering. "What d'you mean, about Laura?"

"That's all I know, but it sounds urgent."

Sophie spun around the slippery mess and half walked, half ran to where the phone sat at the bottom of the main staircase. "Hello. This is Laura's mother. Do you mean Laura Bokum?"

"Yes ma'am. I'm sorry to have to tell you; she's been accused of shooting two people and has escaped. Is your daughter there or do you know where she is?"

"She's not here and no, I don't. She's a police officer and that shooting is being investigated by internal affairs. Why are you calling me now? What do you mean *two* people?"

"Ma'am, regrettably this situation occurred today. We almost apprehended her at the hospital in New Orleans where we understand she was admitting her sister."

"What?" Now Sophie sank down to the bottom stair and her breath became raspy. Almadine stood in front of her and said, "I'll get your inhaler. Stay sitting down."

"Her sister? You mean my other daughter's in the hospital. Why? Why's she in the hospital?"

"I'm sorry to tell you all this over the phone. It must be a terrible shock to you. Give me your address and we'll send an officer over to your home if that'll make you feel better. I'm going to be contacting your local precinct now."

Sophie used all her fingers to wipe the perspiration that'd sprung up on her forehead.

"Here. Inhale." Sophie did as Almadine took the receiver calmly and stated, "Mrs. Clark is asthmatic. Please hang on while she uses her inhaler."

The quick-acting Nebulizer worked its magic and Sophie took the phone back again. "I need to tell you, my husband is a police officer… now detective. His name is Angus Clark. Please ask for him at the precinct."

"Thank you for your cooperation. We'll keep you apprised of any news. Please notify us if you hear from your daughter. The sooner we get a statement from her, the quicker we can clear some of this up."

"I'll call you if I hear from her. No need to send anyone here. Not necessary. Goodbye." *Click*. Sophie pressed the button, ending the call.

Sophie sat looking at the handset, breathing evenly now, just a bit wheezy. Almadine replaced the receiver and sat down next to Sophie on the stair. Sophie spoke slowly. "Laura is accused of shooting two people in New Orleans. Mandy Rose is in the hospital."

"Oh, dear Lord." Almadine made the sign of the cross, then bowed her head. Sophie's head dropped also. The two women sat in a shared stillness; pregnant with the agony of new loss.

CHAPTER 45

Clyde was relieved. His tongue, in spite of all the blood, didn't require stitches. The ice cubes brought down the swelling. He no longer felt like his whole mouth housed a full-grown toad. Tylenol was kicking the headache and the shoulder pain.

The elevator door opened. He exited and heard his name called by a newly recognizable voice. "Clyde. Clyde."

He half mumbled, half thought, "Now what?"

Breathless answer. "She's gone." It was Camille, eyes wild and on a trot.

He put his arm out to stop her from running right into him. "What?"

"It's Mandy's sister, Laura."

"Yeah, what about her?"

"I guess she took off. I didn't want to, but I had to call the cops."

"She is a cop."

"I know, but she shot someone and the cops are on their way."

"Oh fuck, Jesus Christ. Do you know where she was going?"

"No, I don't. I didn't think she'd leave. I had to use the bathroom."

"Where's Mandy Rose?"

"On the psyche ward. She's still not talking."

"Camille, can you get a cab and go home?"

"I don't have a home; only the place that kept me captive. I can't go back there."

"Why?"

"I think they were planning to kill me and maybe Mandy Rose. They only wanted us for our amulets."

Clyde's face opened up. "Amulets? You mean you think they have my gris-gris?"

"Yes, I'm pretty sure they do."

"Why do they want them?"

"For the power. They want to use their power."

"For what?"

Camille swung her hair back off her shoulders and said, "That, I don't know."

Clyde looked at the woman and narrowed his eyes. Something felt off. "Holy shit. You can go to my house. Stay there till you figure something else out."

"Oh my God, thank you, Clyde."

Clyde handed over several twenties and his address. He patted her on the back and smiled as best he could with a tongue still swollen and painful.

She looked into his eyes as hers watered. Her expression was not easily read.

Clyde opted not to visit Mandy Rose on the psyche ward, instead took the stairs to the main lobby of the hospital and set out to track down Laura. The sun had set, making the smokey shadows long and eerie. He had two missions.

Find Laura. Find his gris-gris.

CHAPTER 46

Almadine took a large cotton hanky from her apron pocket and blotted Sophie's eyes, then handed it to her with one word. "Blow."

Sophie did as she was told.

The front door was wide open as Hannah and Arriona entered the cool and spacious front room. Sophie rearranged her face as she handed the damp hanky back to Almadine.

Arriona waved a paper over her head and exclaimed, "One hundred; got all my test words spelled right."

Hannah took a sharp right, headed straight for her room.

"Hannah, come and say hello before you vanish."

Hannah stopped, looked back over her shoulder with slitted eyes and parroted, "Hello."

The grandmother's tears resumed. Sophie wanted a drink in the worst way. She castigated herself. "What on earth is wrong with me? I can't get it right. I love Mandy, Laura and Hannah and all three are messed up."

The ferocious craving for alcohol, for relief, intensified. She headed for the liquor cabinet. The thought rolled over in her brain; Arriona was raised by a single mother with limited funds and was mentally and emotionally stable. She gasped when she got to the liquor cabinet to see Almadine standing guard, arms folded over her ample bosom.

"No Sophie, please. Don't give in to it."

Sophie twisted and bit her lower lip and studied Almadine's serious brown eyes. The warm spirals of affection weren't tainted by any judgmental vibes. Almadine loved Sophie.

"Let's both get us a slice of that key lime pie I made today."

Sophie spun on her sandals and nodded.

Arriona, who'd watched the exchange, went to fetch Hannah to join in on the unexpected afternoon treat. The door to Hannah's room was closed. Not just closed; locked. Arriona raised her slender brown fist to knock. She stopped.

A strange sound was circulating in Hannah's room. A soft insistent moaning. Sounded like Hannah, but not like Hannah.

Bang, bang, bang. "Hannah. Hannah. Are you okay? Open the door. Hannah. Hannah."

Pie forgotten, Sophie and Almadine bolted up the hallway and skidded to a stop where Arriona stood stiff with bent head, rapidly pounding her small fists. Both fists.

Sophie wailed, "Hannah." Her voice cracked with fear of the unknown. She tried again. "Hannah, open the door."

The dogged keening stopped. Two voices could be heard. Sophie clawed at her face and shouted, "Who's in there with you?"

Silence. The air was thick and cloying. Then, almost inaudible, a voice. The voice of Hannah. "I'm alone. What do you all want?"

Sophie leaned closer to the door, her lips touching the smooth wood. "Please come out, Hannah."

The sharp answer. "What do you want? Can't you all leave me alone?"

Sophie sobbed, making tiny bubbly sounds as Almadine tried, "Miss Hannah, come out and have some pie with us. I made it fresh today. One of your favorites, missy. It's key lime."

Inside the room, Hannah made a decision. She pushed some articles to the back floor of her closet and sang out in a syrupy voice. "Be right out."

Sophie, Almadine and Arriona were glad when the door creaked open, still less than appeased that all was well.

Hannah appeared. Her face the epitome of a beatific vision, her eyes dreamy, her lips parted and moist; an other-worldly smile.

All was not well.

CHAPTER 47

"This place needs to be thoroughly searched." The lead detective stood there, legs apart, hands punched into beefy hips. He tried to recall every bit he'd heard about this place. "Voodoos an accepted religion 'round here, but I'm betting more than that witchcraft crap is going on in this place." The two detectives donned pull-on blue rubber gloves and proceeded to open drawers where the woman with the shot-out fingers had sat. Her desk had locks on each of the eight drawers. The center drawer revealed a ring of keys. Two of these proved to be a fit for most of the drawers. One key fit nowhere. One was a skeleton key. The drawers that didn't respond to keys were forced open. Everything was now exposed.

"There's files in here, lots of notebooks."

"That Voodoo stuff? Chants, incantations, spells?" Peterson always liked to give the impression he was "in the know."

"Wait. Don't look like that, sir."

"What does it look like? Never mind, let me see. Grab me a pair of those gloves so I can take a look."

"Yes sir."

Don Peterson moved fast; dug into the box for another pair of gloves, had them in his superior's hands in seconds.

Snap, snap. Gloves stretched on. One gloved hand pulled out a pair of horn-rimmed glasses while the other reached beneath for an open file. "Holy shit. This isn't Voodoo. This is something different. Names and money amounts. I want a seizure order. I want all these books confiscated and moved to headquarters. Derwood, make the call and give me the phone."

"Now, sir?"

"Now, God damn it and make sure that wounded woman doesn't leave the hospital. This is a fricken' cover-up. She knows something."

"Yes, sir. Right away, sir."

"Damn. This is gonna be big."

CHAPTER 48

Clyde touched his fingertips to his mouth. The numbness from the anesthesia injected into his tongue made his lips and chin feel like cement. "Did rigor mortis feel like that?" Still very little sensitivity; a slight tickle; his lips felt a buzzy tingle. He tried to speak. "Now ith the time for all good men to come to the aid of their country."

Not bad. He was hungry and thirsty. Plenty of places to eat. He chose one and looked in the window to make a decision.

"Oh my God. Holy shit." He pushed open the door and stared at a booth where an attractive young woman was forking a hush puppy into puffy pink lips. Without detour, he strode right to her table.

"Mimi," he said as he slid in across from her at the two-person booth.

"Clyde," she blurted, mouth bursting with cornmeal batter.

"You need to exthplain yourthelf."

"I can, Clyde. I'm not what you might be thinking I am. What's the matter with your mouth?"

"Don't change the thubject. I just bit my tongue. Why were you with those animals?"

"It's a long story."

"Try me."

"My father was involved with them for many years, so they knew about me. I saw them all the time when I was little, so they had to keep me close and under their control. I was a danger because I could identify them." She pushed a golden brown, crispy square of cat fish around with her fork.

"Tho, you're not one of them?"

"No, but I'm deathly afraid of them. You should be too." She swallowed and stabbed another hush puppy. She gave him a pitying look. "Did they have anything to do with your split tongue?"

Clyde looked deeper into her eyes. "Yep, good guess. Now will you help me?"

Mimi looked down at her half-empty plate. "I don't think so. No."

Clyde tried again. "Pleath, just tell me the name of whoever's in charge."

"Will you leave me alone then?"

"Yeah, name pleath."

Mimi eyeballed the entire restaurant, swallowed again and whispered, "Jango."

"Jango?"

"Shhhh, shut up! Just Jango, no other name."

Clyde plucked a hush puppy off her plate and popped it into his mouth, intended to let it sit there till it melted. Damn it tasted good. He was so hungry.

He had work to do. He slid out of the bench and touched his fingertips to his lips and opened his palm toward her.

She smiled and hoped no one had seen him with her.

CHAPTER 49

Laura knew the police were looking for her. "Where the hell was Clyde?" As for Camille, Mandy's new little friend; she hoped that one had somewhere to go. "What a mess. At least Mandy was safe, in good hands. Maybe this would be her salvation."

Laura spotted a used clothing store. The sign said "Second Chance." The bell over the door clanged as she entered. An old man, bent over with scoliosis, looked up from a counter with a jumble of small doodads for sale on it next to an ancient cash register. The elderly storekeeper said, "Hiya, miss. Help you?"

"Yes, please. I need a hat with a wide brim and a long-sleeved shirt."

"Hats over there. " He pointed to a shelf that held an amazing number of chapeaus, all stacked up on top of each other. The old man pointed a gnarly finger and said, "Mirror right there." A small round mirror was nailed to a post.

It took Laura less than a minute to find the perfect hat; covered all her ash blonde hair and pulled low over her eyebrows; a nondescript brownish gray. She tucked it under her arm and pawed through the over-blouses that had long sleeves. Bingo again. A size or two too large for her and another grayish garment. She took off her over-blouse and hung it where the grayish one had been. The old guy didn't notice, or he didn't want to. She took her two prizes to the counter. "How much?"

"Ten dollars." She knew she was getting gouged but reached into her pocket, pulled off a wad and peeled off a ten-spot; handed it over.

Outside, she adjusted the hat and did all the buttons on the voluminous shirt. She patted her sidearm and headed into the streets. The ebony blackness of New Orleans nighttime gloom suited her purpose. The occasional wave of red or purple neon lights did little to add some cheer to the tableau.

Back at the house where the earlier shootings took place, she wasn't surprised by the band of crime scene tape. She joined the lookie-loos, stood around slumped over, hands in her pockets and listened. She poked underneath her floppy hat, pushed her hair behind her ears. She wanted to hear what the locals were saying. Hungry for anything that might help unearth these bastards. What was this house hiding? Who were the players? What was their game? Her ears perked up.

"Yes, mm ma'am. That ain't just a Voodoo parlor. I heared they took kids in there."

"No, are you shittin' me?"

"No, not shittin' you. Them two what got shot was bad news."

"You know who shot 'em?"

"Yeah, some chick."

"They catch 'er?"

"Nope, got away."

"Good fer her. Was that big shot in there?"

"What big shot?"

"You know damn well what big shot. They call 'im Jangle or Jingle or sumpthin' like that."

"Hey, shut up. Don't say that too loud you stupid fuck." And now the speaker's voice went low… "Guy's a real dirtbag. His name is…"

Laura watched out of the corner of her eye as the guy looked around furtively, put his pudgy forefinger over his mouth that was buried beneath a gray mustache and beard, that weirdly enough had some mustard yellow color in it. This left little doubt that the name whispered surreptitiously was Jango.

She looked down, getting nervous as the crowd thinned. She left, scuffling away the name burning in her brain.

"Jango."

CHAPTER 50

Laura felt a trickle of sweat make its way down her spine. *I shot two people in that building*. She had to get inside without being noticed.

The structures were all jammed together. Mostly brick buildings, but some had an almost invisible alley between them. Sluffing along at a steady pace; not hurrying, but not dawdling, her face broke into a smile discovering an alley that appeared to lead to the back of the building she wanted to enter. A quick gander under the brim of her hat told her she was being ignored, just a nobody. She twisted sideways and slipped into the dark alley. Her nose dripped as the smells attacked; she pictured dead rats and decaying condoms. A glisten here and there announced plenty of sharp and slimy objects to navigate. *Crunch*; under one foot as the other sought to plant itself farther in. "Arggghhh." She'd stepped on a soft, slippery substance that sent her to her hands and knees. "Christ, this is disgusting." Fury built in her like a volcano, her chest heaving. "Damn you, Mandy Rose."

Then just as swiftly, burning guilt bubbled up. She saw Mandy Rose as she'd left her. Alone and psychotic. Laura struggled with the knowledge that their father had molested Mandy from the time she was a little girl. But not her. Why not her?

This question tortured her.

Clamping her teeth together, she spoke out loud to the filthy feces-infested alley. "I wish I believed in Hell, 'cause that's where you belong dear daddy; to burn and suffer for eternity."

Now her everpresent, but not always recognized, guiding force kicked in. "The Watcher." "Focus Laura, let go of the anger. Remember your mission."

Good thing because a fat gray rat charged out of a dark spot, it's pointy nails making rapid tapping sounds as it scurried up the alley in front of Laura, its fat little ass trailing a long naked tail.

Laura stopped, stood, tightened her stomach and loins, ready to proceed. Now aware of the sewage underfoot as her eyes adjusted she could make better decisions about where to place her next step. Many others played and paid in this alley. Condoms lay white and flattened and whisky bottles were brown and empty.

Coming to the back of the building, she was surprised to see there was no crime scene tape. No signs this entrance had been used. Laura took out a bobby pin and after several tries knew it wouldn't serve the purpose. "Damn it." Next, she pulled out her bump key from her back pocket; never tried except at academy. Her last hope. She'd filed it down, almost removing all the cut edges but not losing the shapes. She wished she'd tested it. Now was not the time for regrets.

Her vision acclimated, and she could make out shapes. She pushed the bump key into the lock, right up to the last pin. She listened for a series of soft clicks. Yes. The pins were lifted by the key; allowing the tumblers that kept the door secure to be moved out of the way. Now the tricky part. Stop pushing the key. Strike it. Strike it hard and turn the key fast. Tumbler should swivel and the door should open. Should.

She slammed it with the heel of her hand. Nothing. Second try. Repeat the procedure. Door remained locked. Ah, she spotted a smooth stone, just fist size; perfect. Holding the key inserted, she bent down to grab it. Barely, but yes. She backed up her elbow with the stone. One more try. Ready. *Wham*! Success. The tumbler swiveled. The door opened. She stepped inside.

The smell was goat leavings, fire place smudge and her overdeveloped olfactory sense screamed; blood.

The place was empty. She continued stepping lightly, making as little noise as possible. The room with the bed where she'd encountered her sister and Camille looked different. Stripped of all bedding and goat bones and of course, the body of the brute she'd shot earlier made her swallow a tablespoon of spit that invaded her mouth. Maybe it was bile.

She followed the hallway into the front room. The fancy room where she'd shot the woman sitting at her desk. A good call. That woman would've called her goons. And maybe shot her, Mandy Rose and Camille. Laura said out loud, "Nah, I would've gotten at least one more of them."

The desk drawers all stood open and empty. But Laura was thorough. She bent down under the desk and ran her hand all around the underside. Fingers stretching, searching. Yes! Way back by the edge a piece of tape held a small elongated hard object. Her fingernail plucked at the tape's cut end till it gave way and the thing fell, hung there.

"The Watcher" knew and went on alert. Laura slid the slender find out. Immediately exaggerated olfactory senses came alive. She smelled evil. The scent of death. She sat on the floor and took *it* out to inspect it. She let it tumble into her cupped hands and gasped. It burned her palms. It was hot. It screamed, "Possession." It was a bone. A bone! She let it fall right there. It made a high-pitched tinkling sound. Like a tiny scream. She scrambled to her feet ready to run.

She wanted out of there. Right now.

Footsteps coming down the hallway. Someone had come through her burgled door. The heavier sounds and length of tread; likely a man. A tall man. A lean man. With dim light shining on the features, Laura recognized the body build. A loud sigh. "Ahhhh." A single word.

"Clyde."

CHAPTER 51

"Almadine, where's Sophie?"

"Mister Clark sir, she wasn't feeling so good."

"Almadine, please call me Angus. Where is she?"

"Mister, uh, Angus sir, Missus Sophie went up to take a nap; said her head hurt."

"I don't know the best way to say this, but was she was uh… you know." Angus tipped a fist up to his mouth and mimicked drinking a liquid.

"No sir, not that. She was upset about Laura."

"Yes, I know about Laura. There's a bulletin out for her." Angus mopped his brow. "I know Laura. I'm sure there's a very good explanation."

"Maybe so, Angus sir, but Sophie got to crying so bad, she had to lie down."

"Thank you, Almadine. I don't know what this family would do without you."

Angus stepped lightly, went up to his and Sophie's bedroom. He was greeted with a darkened room, all draperies closed up. He gently pushed the door open. He could see Sophie's golden curls spread out on the lavender pillow. The concerned husband heard her somewhat raspy breathing. His heart ached for the increased size of the mound on the bed moving up and down. He knew she'd been upset with her weight gain. Now Mandy Rose and Laura were both in shaky situations, Sophie needed his support more than ever.

He moved silently to the bed and edged in next to her, placed his hand on her shoulder. "Sophie, Sophie honey." His voice was low and tender. She jolted. Her body twisted. Angus could see the residue the salty tears made on her flushed cheeks.

"Angus. Oh, Angus."

"It's all right, honey. I have news; most of it good."

Now she pushed herself up and wiped her face with the hanky she'd taken back from Almadine.

"We have a positive identification from the two teenage boys who saw the sisters that were abducted. This could lead to another location where they take these children."

Sophie's eyes widened. "You mean where Hannah might've gone before her…" She hated saying the word but managed, "adoption?"

"Yes, exactly that."

Sophie's eyes brimmed with hot new tears as thoughts of Hannah caved in on her. She laid her head on Angus's chest.

His tender heart broke for her, made his chest feel full as though it couldn't contain any more pain. He rubbed her back.

"This may help us understand what we're dealing with, with Hannah."

Her shoulders tightened. She lifted her head and spoke. "You're right. Let's go get some lemonade and you can tell me everything."

Angus marveled at her ability to find strength in the midst of all the turmoil. He took her hand and pulled her out of the bed, glad to see she was fully dressed, ready to go downstairs, drink lemonade and talk things out.

He reached under the bed and held out two golden sandals for her. He knelt as she slipped her feet into them.

"Ready Cinderella?"

"Ready Prince Charming."

CHAPTER 52

"Okay, what've we got here?" The stout nurse adjusted her midriff and said, "Doctor Montgomery, she was admitted like this after a bout of florid activity."

"Explain what you mean by florid? Don't use terms unless you're sure of their meaning."

"Sorry, Doctor. I mean she wasn't quiet like this. She was screaming and combative."

"Combative, how?"

"She was striking out with closed fists and kicking. She was subsequently put in constraints and administered Haldol by injection.

"How much Haloperidol?"

"Five mgs, starter, then five mgs again."

"Has she said anything?"

"Nothing that makes much sense. Something like "little girl" and "but, it hurts."

"Who brought her in?"

"That's the strange part. Two women brought her here. One a friend. The other, her sister who, we discovered, is wanted by the police."

"Where are they?"

"Both gone."

"All right. Move away and let me examine her." The psychiatrist leaned over Mandy Rose's supine form with intentions of checking to see if her pupils were dilated. As he bent closer, his hand lifted with its exploratory pen light, but it never made it to Mandy's eyes which sprang open with rounded terror, whites showing, as the good doctor's forelock dumped over close to Mandy's face.

She shrieked loud enough to cause the dead to burst from their coffins. Unable to defend herself due to the restraints, she swung her shoulders left to right, over and over, then started bucking with her head, striking Doctor Montgomery's forehead with a solid *thunk*. He leaped back.

"Ow. Give her another five mgs and put her in a room to let her scream it out. She's totally psychotic. Nothing I can do for her right now. I'll check on her tomorrow."

"But Doctor, she might need water, or food, or to relieve herself?"

"Are you questioning me?"

"No sir, I was just…"

"Just nothing. Do what I said. And five more mgs of Haldol every four hours."

"Yes, Doctor." The nurse sucked in her top lip.

Doctor Montgomery swung his long slender body on his three-hundred-dollar Italian loafers and left the cubicle.

The nurse prepared the next dose of Haldol. She jabbed Mandy Rose's arm, pushed the plunger right through the canvas restraint, then left to get coffee and hopefully a beignet to warm in the nuker. She pushed thoughts of the tiny psychotic woman away, hoping to drown the vision in caffeine and sugar.

A dark room. Mandy lay alone in a drugged sleep, breathing in and out. "*Ahhhh, whoosh. Ahhhh, whoosh.*"

Then there were three.

"Hey Junior, do you see what I see?"

"Hell yeah; tasty little piece of ass."

The two orderlies crept closer to the slumbering woman. "What the hell happened to her? That's a bad haircut."

Boulder always had the answers. "Nah, nuts often butch their hair, cut it all off; maybe a substitute for offing themselves."

"Shit Boulder, you're really smart."

"Yeah, I know. Help me get this blanket down so we can see what we got here."

"'Kay, go slow. I wanna make it like a striptease."

The two men, both in their twenties and both tall and skinny, each took a corner of the pale yellow coverlet and rolled it down to the bottom of the bed; which was little more than a cot.

"Holy shit, she's skinny."

"Yeah, but young. We can't undo the straight jacket, so we can't see her boobs."

"Yeah, but everything else is right there in front of us."

Junior bent over for a closer look and drooled a long string of spittle onto Mandy Rose's naked thigh.

"Who goes first?"

"Should we just play with her a little bit for now and come back later for the full treatment?"

Boulder's eyes were shiny with lust, but he knew Junior made sense. "You're right, Juney, just get a little taste with your finger or your tongue and let's get outta here. They'll drug her up more and won't check on her later tonight."

Junior was already enjoying himself.

"Awright, get your head out of there and let me have a taste."

Just then the night time hall lights switched on and bathed the corridor in a sickly yellow. Junior jerked straight up, holding on to the front of his pants while Boulder bent low. Now Boulder grasped the front of his overalls also. Boulder licked his lips. "Fuck, she is sweet. Pull the cover back up and let's boogie."

Mandy Rose, almost comatose, was largely unaware she'd been visited.

CHAPTER 53

Laura was glad to have Clyde with her. They'd never go back to being lovers. That was fine. She still had her eye on that tall dark and handsome rookie. After everything got cleared up and if he wasn't freaked now over her use of firearms, she'd ask him out.

She showed Clyde her macabre find.

Clyde held the tiny bone up to the light that drifted in through a high dusty window. "This may be some kind of a clue. It has to be important or it wouldn't have been hidden."

Laura started, "Yeah, you don't hide anything that well, unless…" She stopped. Her mouth dropped. She caste a gaze upward and to the right.

Clyde noticed. "What is it, did you…" He was struck dumb. His body undulated and trembled. The little bone forgotten, he pressed his right hand to his heart and stayed silent.

Both were feeling the sound and energy of ten thousand bees as they waited for more intelligence to appear. Clyde began a rolling, deep throated chant. "Mama Beee Yan Ka. Mamma Beee Yan Ka."

Laura got guidance from "The Watcher." The message was that Mandy Rose was in danger.

Clyde's head dropped to his chest and his fists balled at his sides. This chant wasn't consciously familiar to him. How could he know it was the name Mandy Rose had chosen for herself.

Laura gave Clyde a rough shove in the middle of his chest, making his head pop up. Now he was on the same wave length as her. "It's Mandy, isn't it?"

"Yes, we have to get back to that hospital."

They raced out the way they'd entered, burst onto the hot and humid street, hell bent on getting to Mandy Rose.

Mandy Rose was in trouble.

132

Oh! Where was his gris-gris. How long could he "coast" on residual energy from his grandfather's amulet? The stray thought flitted through his mind. *Has my daughter inherited the power of our family totem? Could that be what ails Hannah?* He loved his daughter and he loved her mother.

He pushed all this aside and hailed a taxi, which skidded to a stop on the curb in front of Laura. Was their combined power helping? They hopped in, gave the destination and roared off. They were a team. He recalled how Mandy had broken him out of the mental institution, and now they were planning to do the same thing for her. Break her out.

It would be dark, fewer staff and likely no doctors. Laura knew how to get past locks. He knew how with one punch to take out anyone who blocked their way.

The cab skidded to the main entrance. Laura whispered, "Walk like you belong here. Don't run."

Clyde threw his shoulders back and leaned into Laura, looking for all the world like a doctor in street clothes discussing a patient with a family member.

They completely ignored the middle-aged woman at the front desk who appeared bored as she played with one of her pearl earrings. She looked up and dismissed the handsome couple as of no interest or threat.

They knew where Mandy Rose had been taken and found themselves facing a locked door to that wing. Laura made short work of it. Clyde smiled at her expertise. They continued down the corridor, each taking a side to look into the mostly occupied rooms. All the beds had yellow coverlets that moved up and down as the hapless people slept and breathed in their captivity.

Mandy's shorn locks made her easy to spot.

Something was wrong. Different. Suspicious. All the other patients had the blankets tucked in on both sides of their slim beds.

Not Mandy's. Her blanket was pulled free and wrinkled at the top.

"Someone was in here." Clyde's face took on a menacing expression. His brows crammed together and his forehead scrunched to meet them. He clamped his teeth down so violently his tongue shoved a trickle of blood over the corner of his lip.

Laura said, "Calm down, that won't help. Let's get her outta here." She undid the ties on the straitjacket and gave a quick rub to her sister's wrists to bring back circulation.

Someone was coming. Two someones.

A shadow draped over the doorway and announced the degenerates; back to rape Mandy Rose. So full of their prurient plans, they took too long to notice their prey wasn't alone.

Clyde had no problem guessing their despicable mission. While Laura worked to get Mandy on her feet, Clyde took action. He sucker punched the pug-faced guy; blood spurted from his nose, then he next gave a sound upper cut to the bug-eyed guy who cried out, "Fuck." But he never got another word out. Clyde slammed his fist into the scrawny giant's face. The sound of a broken nose filled the little room as bright crimson blood spurted onto Clyde's fist.

Both men, though tall, were built delicately and appeared to be down for the count.

"Can she walk?"

"Yeah, if we keep her up."

Mandy's eyes were half open, her lids swollen from the neuroleptics. She managed a crooked smile. "My shart."

"What?" Laura asked. "Oh, she's right, Clyde. Take her chart. It's on the bottom of the bed."

Clyde stuffed it in his pocket and said, "I'll hold Mandy. You get their coats off them. Tell me if they start to wake up."

"Good idea." Laura, stronger than she looked, wrestled both of the hospital-issue jackets off the fallen cretins.

Closing the door behind them, the motley trio headed up the hall, through the still unlocked door that looked the same as it had when they'd left it. Next, they entered the front lobby. The same woman leaned on her hand, fast asleep, her hair sprung from its fastenings.

They hurried out the main entrance.

Clyde had them all in a cab, heading for his little house where he knew Camille would be waiting. She could watch over Mandy Rose while he and Laura continued to search for answers.

Clyde wondered if he would be able to get into the police academy.

They *were* quite a team.

CHAPTER 54

Inside a bedroom, inside an enormous mansion, perched on the edge of a bed, a hand-mirror held inches from her face, Hannah stared into her own emerald green eyes. Her gaze burrowed deeper, searching for answers. Nothing moved on her young slim body. Only her raspberry curls floated adrift, teased by the overhead fan that whirled unceasingly.

Her image fascinated her. She was entranced. The heat and color of a house in flames around her wouldn't reach the girl's physical senses in time to save her life.

The mirror image wavered. Metamorphosed. Now she gaped, seeing a much older visage. The saliva in her mouth dried up in seconds. Her cinnamon curls darkened, became black and velvety, poking out from a midnight blue turban. The locks lay on a very high, cocoa colored forehead. Deep dark eyes were fringed with velvety black lashes. And though heavily lidded, the eyes pierced Hannah's very soul. The aquiline nose, noble and elegant, differed from the usual tiny pug feature. High, almost sharp cheekbones completed the vision. The little girl's naked lips were now swollen and pouty, a ruby color so ebony they resembled glistening coal.

Hannah was paralyzed, transfixed.

The image in the mirror stirred provocatively. Movement. Hannah's eyes rounded as the clinging circuitous shape around the mirror image's face materialized. Around the neck; a snake. A yellow eely thing with green markings.

Hannah's terror diminished. Her mirror twin smiled. An enigmatic smile showed milky-white teeth, a striking contrast to the ebony lips. Hannah's trance-like state loosened. She observed the phenomenon and stayed connected with her mundane faculties intact. A dual state of consciousness, not new to her. She felt unable to speak, glued to the spot where she sat.

The woman smiled, broadly now. She knew Hannah'd acclimated to her presence. It was time to speak to the child. None of this would involve physical speech. Only telepathy.

Hannah closed her eyes, felt a burgeoning of maturation, aging in years in mere minutes. She prepared herself for the messages intended for her and her alone.

A sound. A melody blossomed. The inner sound correlating to the physical sense of sound that used physical ears. A group of words in a bolt of telepathic energy pushed aside the eerie music.

No sound now, other than the paddling of the ceiling fan endlessly circling.

"You are in danger my child. You are being sought by those who would commandeer your powers for evil purpose. These beings will attempt to seize the gifts you are entitled to through your father and your grandfather and your grandfather's mother. You are the first female born into this line of Houngans and Mambos. Your powers will surpass everything known within the past hundred years; exceeding anything possible by your male ancestors. You are destined to be a High Priestess."

"Wicked men know this. They search for you even as I speak."

Hannah knew she had only to think her questions to be "heard" and understood. "What should I do?"

"You must acknowledge your father and seek his wisdom. He is the only force at your immediate disposal against these depraved evil men. They'll use your powers against you, forcing you to choose lesser evils in situations that involve other human beings. They are not without some power."

Hannah felt scared but also relieved. She'd been wrestling with the dueling demons, not feeling adequate to handle all the conflicting impressions; some so dark, she wanted to kill herself or worse, kill someone else… maybe Arriona. "What do I do?"

"You must wait. Your father was searching for your mother. She's now found. I'll contact you again my child. The same method."

"No, don't go. I'm scared." The image began to break into tiny fragments. The little puzzle pieces floated away from the rim of the handheld mirror and nothing remained but a white fog. Hannah waited until her familiar face returned.

She saw herself while her eyes were still shuttered. She looked pale. Both eyes blinked then opened. The image crystalized.

The fan slowed down. Its speed having been sped up by the overload of energy, now gone.

Hannah pictured her father's face and felt a warm spot grow in her little girl's chest. It was time to know him.

CHAPTER 55

"Clark! In my office. Now."

Angus left the cup of coffee he'd just brought in on his desk to cool. Thinking it must be something big, he lengthened his stride and was almost on Rick Sloane's heels when he entered the captain's office.

"Shut the door behind you and sit."

Angus didn't argue, plopped down. Captain Sloane's face was red, his jaw tight with some as yet unknown resolve. Angus waited. He leaned forward, wanting to hear every word.

Still standing, Rick grabbed the edge of his desk and jutted his head toward Angus. The two law enforcement officers were two feet apart. "For starters, your daughter, Laura…"

Angus knew better than to correct the family connection.

Sloane continued. "I should say, your wife's daughter is still on the loose. The story keeps getting worse. She's being pursued by NOLA and so far has managed to elude them. Here's where we combine jurisdictions; the call I had this morning informed me that they have documents detailing illegal activity concerning children and others. We still have more questions than answers. This rot goes deep. I believe Laura is still "on the job." I also believe IA will clear her of all wrong doing." Rick fell into his chair. His face relaxed a bit.

"Okay, Rick. What do you want me to do?"

"I want to know whatever she knows. Has she contacted your wife?"

"No. Well, not that I know of."

"All right. There's more to this story. It seems three people left the building where Laura shot and killed a man. She also shot a woman's hand. We tracked the cab from that time, location and description of the people. Three women to be exact. They were dropped off at the emergency room entrance at the nearby hospital."

Angus frowned as he tried to untangle all this. Could that be Mandy

Rose and Laura and some unknown other woman? He looked straight at Rick and stated again, "What do you want me to do?"

Sloane answered with another question. "Do you know where that guy, Clyde Boudreaux, is?"

Angus's turn to answer with a question. "Why? Do you think he's involved?"

Rick Sloane passed his palm across his forehead and looked away. Angus repeated, "Do you think Boudreaux's involved?"

A heavy silence fell on the room.

At last Sloane spoke. "Do you believe in Voodoo?"

Angus pulled into himself as a slight tremor sadistically claimed his body. Afraid to say it out loud, it shook his very soul. He gasped. "Hannah."

CHAPTER 56

Hannah felt urges. Power that threatened to take over her whole being. One minute she trembled with something close to fear, but not fear; more a premonition. A catastrophe coming toward, no, not toward; away from her. The stark reality was she felt the terror of wanting to recoil from her own self. Dread. The horror of what was coming. Coming from her. A ghastly tsunami. It would only crescendo when she went where she was destined to go. In the ancient cards; predicted from its source in deepest darkest Africa. It was her fate to acknowledge what she was and embrace it. To use it. It was her destiny.

Now she was aware; knew she had to follow the path laid out for her by her ancestors. Yes, she was young to accept the crown; the title. She had to bridge the distance to where her energized amulets and sacred objects were stored. She was the new queen.

Glad everyone in the house seemed preoccupied, not looking for her.

Evening was enveloping the mansion. The last meal was long over. Almadine was through cleaning up and already in her room. Hannah feared Almadine. That woman knew things. More than she ever let on. Hannah'd spotted a string around the woman's neck that disappeared under her often brightly colored dresses. She suspected the slight bulge between the housekeeper's breasts was a totem. Likely related to Almadine's family and African roots. Probably not very powerful but more animated than anything the pure white folks in the house were privy to.

Hannah stripped down to her underwear, knelt and reached into her closet. She pulled out the doll she'd made and flattened it into her underpants. Next she dragged on a long gray skirt that hung to her skinny ankles. A caramel-colored pullover made of a light-weight burlap went over her head. She smoothed it out. It totally camouflaged the buried doll. The pockets were wide and deep. Perfect. From a hook in her closet, she grabbed a braided rope and tied it loosely around her waist. Money in this house was never a problem. There were piles of cash everywhere. No one ever worried about theft. The only people who spent time in the house, besides Sophie, was Almadine, and of course, Cedric, the chauffeur. Hannah regretted assuming he'd take advantage of her when she baited him. She almost wanted him to be bad. She didn't trust men. Any men. Horrible flashbacks of the time she'd spent in that awful warehouse before she got sent to be adopted. She gave a quick thought to those people. Her adoptive parents. Nope, she didn't belong in New Jersey; being raised like a pampered, spoiled white girl.

She knew now that Clyde was her daddy. Yes, and what a daddy he was. Right now, she'd find her way to his little house and his *special* room. Her heart beat like a djembe drum. Her African roots were alive and firing up her religious fervor. A ritual *boom boom boom* took over her heart's rhythm.

Time to go. She slipped into her huaraches; smiled remembering how surprised and happy her grandmother was to take her shopping for these unusual sandals. Sophie'd found it odd but complied.

Hannah, not wanting to turn on any lights, left her room and felt her way down the hallway. Her huaraches made the tiniest whisper of noise. Into the great room and relying on past habits, she opened the cabinet where the liquor was stored and slipped her hand under a pile of paper currency. A lot of money.

She had to make it to the front door without being discovered. *Whisper, whisper, whisper.* Reaching her immature and slender hand toward the door, she pulled on the ornate handle with four fingers. The small girl slipped through the narrow opening and into a balmy, humid star-studded night. Breaking into a leisurely trot, she headed to where she could take a bus into a small town. An area where a taxi could be had. She didn't dare risk using the phone to have a cab come to the mansion.

Dropping a five-dollar bill into the bus driver's hand, she said, "Town please."

The big-bellied middle-aged white driver gave her a questioning look but said nothing. He gave her change.

She sat on a hard green seat next to an old woman who used both knobby hands to hold tightly to a crocheted pocketbook with huge tortoise shell handles that clacked as the bus took off. The old crone stroked the handles lovingly.

Hannah smiled to herself. Soon she'd be giving a cabby her father's address.

Soon she'd be where she craved to be.

Craved like a hungry animal.

A hungry lion who'd only be satisfied with a feast. A feast of others. Her lips curled up as she savored the thoughts of the work she'd already begun.

CHAPTER 57

Hannah gave short answers to the cab driver. "Are you sure that's where you want to go, little lady?"

"Yes, I'm sure."

"That's kinda a dangerous part of town. Not too many white people live there. Did you know that?"

Laconically, she said, "Yes."

"None of my business, but if you want me to wait for you, like you said… the meter keeps running."

"I know that." Hannah was very patient with the taxi driver.

"Cost you a bundle, sweetheart."

Hannah grimaced at the inappropriate endearment. Didn't want to acknowledge it with an answer.

"Missy, did you hear me?"

"I heard."

The small girl watched out the window. The accumulated dust made mud when she spit at it and wiped it with her hanky. Visibility was waning as the sky turned purple. The taxi bumped and grumbled as the street became less friendly. The smooth surface disappeared. Fifteen minutes later, the cab came upon a small house. It was little more than a shack. Hannah leaned forward to ogle the place through the windshield when the car's driver slammed on the breaks, heaving her into the space between the front seats. "Take a look at that meter girl. It's gonna keep adding to the cost. Maybe you should give me some money up front?"

Hannah peeled off two twenty-dollar bills and dropped them on the front passenger seat.

The man's eyes bulged.

"Don't leave this spot. Wait right here. I won't be long."

He grabbed the Andrew Jacksons, raised his hips and crumpled them into his front pocket.

She opened the back door and slid out. The place looked uncared for and lonely. Nobody to watch over it. The front yard, while mostly dirt, had patches of coarse grass growing in clumps. She wasn't doubtful whether she could gain entry. Her hand reached out for the knob on the front door and in one motion twisted and turned till the inside lay exposed. One foot then the other and the living room was breached.

Having heard all the stories, she knew the round dark blotch on the threadbare carpet was where her father was shot by Felix. Felix left him for dead.

She went gently toward it and bent down close. She laid her palm on it. Then she smelled it, taking in the scent and savoring the whoosh of power that riddled her; a transfusion from her daddy.

Next, a few steps got her into the tiny kitchen; the counter where the poison had sat that killed Bertie Bergeron. She smoothed the floor with the ball of her foot, imagining Hurtie Bertie's chubby body in a dead pile right where she stood.

God, she loved her father.

Time to explore. Down the hall, past the door to all the secrets; choosing to visit the bedroom first. The bed looked like it was bunched up in a rat's nest. The yellowish sheet convulsed. She yelped. Something escaped from under it. "Ahhhh." God damn. A water rat. No, two water rats. "Enough. Nothing here to see."

She retraced her steps and came to the door she'd sought. With a religious reverence, she pushed the door open and closed it all the way behind her. Inside, it was dark. Bits and pieces in the corners sparkled. There was no light source she could decipher.

She wanted to see more. She craved all of it. Out of her capacious pocket, she extracted a short black stump of a candle and wooden matches. Using her thumbnail she flicked the sulfur head that sparked and exploded, then touched the red and yellow flame to the blackened wick.

The room was now in a flickering glow; blinking in and out. Forms revealed themselves in unabashed glory; the Catholic statues of the Virgin Mary smiled.

Hannah pulled her doll out from her underwear and placed it next to three other dolls that had similar markings. She wasn't surprised that her doll mimicked the dolls here in her father's chapel. She moved around, touching this and that as all the dolls watched. The red drum had dark smeared skin stretched over its head. She tapped it seven times. She refused to conjecture the origin of the brown covering. Didn't matter. She knew.

She laid her cheek sensuously to the cheek of a black mask made of polished wood that was pinioned to the wall. Her mind careened. Her muscles, blood and bone were on fire. A spiritual awakening so strong and tender it threatened to propel her out of the bag of skin that enclosed her young body.

A tidy hill of skulls caught her attention. Most were intact, some had missing pieces of bone, leaving sharp openings around the eye sockets. A tall black warrior holding a bejeweled staff caught her eye for a minute until a flash and a sound like a tornado stopped her heart.

The ceiling erupted with activity. Letters. Big bold red letters, all in capitals. She leaned back to read the message.

"Relay the Force Pattern as a Source of Tension…"

Her brow pulled together and her jaw tightened. An insistent noise broke into her reverie. An offensive bleating.

It was time to go. The damn cabby was going ballistic. *Honk, honk, honk.*

Hannah wet her forefinger and thumb and snuffed the candle. She backed out and closed the door. She wanted to get back to the mansion before anyone discovered she'd gone missing.

But she'd be back.

CHAPTER 58

Hannah told the cabby to take her all the way home. It was too late to use the bus, and everyone would be asleep at the house.

The driver was intrigued with his pretty young passenger. His furtive glances aimed at her reflection in the rearview mirror weren't lost on her. She'd learned a long time ago to choose her battles so pretended she didn't notice. She also felt no fear as her energy could be multiplied if she allowed her anger to have free range. Regular mortals were oblivious to unofficial reality. They were clueless to any awareness that they were multi-dimensional and more powerful in their ability to create their worlds, instead seeing themselves as vulnerable beings whose experiences seemed to happen to them. They believed themselves to be victims, subject to the objective world. They none the less, in their ignorance, could be pains in the asses. Hannah smiled as these thoughts circulated in her brain.

"I've never gone down this road before, sweetie."

Sweetie, she thought. *Christ.* "Don't worry. You're fine. Let me off after this next row of trees."

It was dark as black velvet now, and the yellow headlight beams threw a urine-colored path up a well-tended road. The mansion, less than a quarter of a mile up this road, wasn't visible yet.

"Stop here and let me off."

"I can take you the rest of the way. Seems dangerous to drop you off here, little lady."

"I'm fine. Let me off here. Right here."

"Are you sure? I'm not really comfortable…"

Hannah was losing patience. Her voice increased in volume and went deeper; the voice of a fully grown woman. "I said right here."

The cabby's head jolted back, twisting to see if someone else had replaced the little girl in the back seat. He knew that was crazy thinking, but what the…

Hannah spoke again, amending her delivery. "Please sir, just let me off here." Now she'd play the silly game to placate the man, give him an explanation. "If our Doberman hears your engine, she'll bark and wake everyone up."

While the cabby was still perplexed, he wanted to get away. This kid was weird.

Hannah took two fifty dollar bills out of her pocket and rolled them up separately like cigarettes. She leaned forward and as before dropped them into the front passenger seat, saying, "Keep the change."

The cab lurched and heaved up as he yanked the emergency brake. He was clearly freaked out.

She flew out of the vehicle and covered the remaining road at a brisk pace. Entry into the mansion went smoothly and once in her bedroom, she removed the pillows she'd left on her bed, replicating her sleeping form.

She was energized. She was exhilarated; thrilled with the possibilities of discovery. Her potential for mind-blowing power was becoming known to her. It was only the beginning. Would she use it for good? Or evil?

The sentence on the ceiling came back to her. A buzzing sound, then an overpowering urge to look up. Across the ceiling, her bedroom ceiling, in red block letters were the words again.

"Relay the Force Pattern as a Source of Tension..."

She lay, fully clothed on her bed. Plans for her future bubbled.

The possibilities were endless.

The probabilities achievable.

She whispered, "Thank you, Daddy."

CHAPTER 59

Not ready to go to Clyde's, Camille fingered the cash in her pocket. She was finally a free agent and had some money. If she could get her gris-gris back, she'd restore her power. And who knew… maybe the grand prize would be there also. Mandy Rose was oblivious, not a clue of what she'd had in her possession. The gris-gris that belonged to Clyde Boudreaux and before him, Clyde's granddaddy, occupied the pinnacle of Voodoo power. The absolute apex. And now that there was a female involved in the ancestry line, nothing would trump that.

Mandy Rose's daughter was destined to be High Priestess. The gang of deplorables wouldn't stop till they found the girl. Found and took Hannah.

Camille knew that once early childhood had spent itself the power grew and asserted its hold on the female next in line. It would be tripled or more since a girl child had been missing for so long. But no more. Now there was Hannah.

Camille took a maroon kerchief from her pocket and tied it around her forehead, leaving a long tail to droop down her back. Next, she rolled her pants legs up until they were Bermuda shorts. Tearing her sleeves from her shirt, she connected them and made a scarf that went around her neck. She looked different.

She hailed a cab and gave the driver an address.

Ten minutes later she was on the correct street and ecstatic enough to turn cartwheels. The unobtrusive little candy store was deserted. Sandwiched as it was between two larger brick buildings, no one would guess it was where the gang, led by Jango, kept their stash; all their secrets.

Oof. She hoisted her skinny body up to where a window stood closed but not locked. She knew this would be the case from overhearing a conversation about this very dereliction of duty as a security measure.

Her bony little fist pounded the dirt-encrusted swing window. It made a heart-stopping screech. She froze. Camille recalled Doc Stone insisting that no human being could fit through this opening. He was called Doc Stone, 'cause he always complained about his kidney stones.

Luckily her weight was ninety pounds, drenched. She was strong and wiggled her slender hips to gain a lurch up. Now her upper body hung into the room. It was dark. Her legs still flapped around outside the building. Opting to use gravity, she draped over until the weight distribution shifted. She fell with a *thump*, banging her elbow and one flattened hand. She stood and wiped her hands on her homemade Bermuda shorts.

Leaning against a wall to her left were at least a dozen long guns. They stared ominously at her; soldiers looking for a battle.

She rubbed her hurt elbow and walked to the safe. It was, as she figured, one of those old wooden chests covered with pieces of sheet iron, banded and strapped. The slender woman knelt in front of it, then smelled the ancient metal. It made her nose drip.

Camille was ready for this. In her former life, she'd been a safe cracker. And she was good.

The petite woman put her ear near the round knob and using her right hand, still stinging from her floor dive, she slowly, oh so slowly, twisted the knob to the left, counter clockwise and waited. There it was. *Click*. Now clockwise three times to the right. *Click*. She smiled, let her nose drip, not wanting to break the spell. Okay, two times to the left, another soft, barely audible *click*. She wiped her nose with her forearm and continued. Right turning twist till it stopped, not opened yet. Then ever so slowly to the right. The last *click* stopped her breath. She took both hands away for a second and stared at the lever that hung waiting.

Now, fast, she grabbed it, swung it open. She peered into the darkened interior. There were three objects. The two in the back were silent; one was dull, one shone delicately, a soft almost imperceptible glow. That one was hers. Her totem taken over a year ago.

The one in front was *It*. Had to be. It screamed with the volume of a New Year's Eve blast at Times Square. It shrieked at her. Her face shone.

The light that poured out blinded her; like looking directly into a noonday sun.

Camille knew the observer always affected the observed. She was cold but soaked in sweat. What had she done? She needed to act. She had to lift these powerful totems out of this safe. She clutched at her neck, sank back upon her haunches. Fear gained a hold on her. She doubted her knowledge was sufficient to do what she was doing. She wasn't sure what she was up against with the gris-gris from Clyde's granddaddy.

Some gris-gris were dark and sinister, able to deliver evil capable of killing and worse. Many were symbols of spiritual protection. Which were these? She'd carried her own gris-gris in a special pocket she'd made on her belly. Mandy Rose said she'd carried the one she had on her person also. The third amulet was an unknown.

Not willing to risk her life; she vacillated, then decided. She reached in and reclaimed her property, held it lovingly in her palm. The remaining two still a mystery to her.

Camille had to take a chance. The one in front blinked, a harsh whispering sound she wasn't sure she was hearing said, "Take me. Take me."

She closed her fingers around her own totem and slid it into her pocket. Then taking a deep breath, she slipped her other hand under the one she felt must surely be Mandy's. Well, Clyde's. The third gris-gris still sat there.

A noise behind her. A door creaked open. The smell of alcohol.

"What'dyah think you're doing?" a deep gruff voice demanded.

She closed her hand on Clyde's gris-gris and spun to face the intruder and held the amulet up, still blinking and screaming. She aimed it at him. The brute, a massive hulk of a man, widened his eyes and clutched at his shirt front. His mouth made a lopsided oh as he tumbled to the filthy floor, spittle dripping from his lips. She could smell the fear erupting from the mountainous form. His top lip twitched and his eyes rolled back in his head, white and staring. Now the stench from him overpowered her.

Camille wasn't waiting to see what happened next.

The door stood open.

She pocketed Clyde's gris-gris, stepped around the inert body and disappeared into the night.

Tonight, dead tired, she'd rent an SRO and sleep in NOLA.

Tomorrow she'd go to Clyde's.

CHAPTER 60

"I'm hungry." Laura and Clyde ogled each other over Mandy Rose's head, surprised and pleased to hear her speak.

"Okay, let's get some vittles." Clyde smiled broadly, looking obscenely handsome.

Laura tilted her head and puckered her lips. *Damn. He still prefers Mandy.* Her smile froze then closed down.

"Can you get her to walk without her toes buckling?"

"Doesn't matter where we're going."

"Where *are* we going?"

"Where they serve great fried catfish and prize-worthy hush-puppies."

Getting to the restaurant was a minor challenge. But people in NOLA weren't fazed by young women who were being held aloft by their armpits.

Mimi's favorite restaurant was half empty. The waitress waived her flabby arm over several booths, indicating for them to take their choice. They took the one closest to the wall, stuffing Mandy Rose into it as deeply as they could. Her foot caught on the booth's leg and Laura crawled under to disentangle it; aghast at how thin her sister was. Her ankle was the size of a wrist.

The waitress appeared, smacking her lips as she finished eating a greasy something or other. She wiped her shiny fingers on her apron then pulled out an order pad in one motion. "What can I get you all?"

Clyde looked at Laura with raised eyebrows. She said to the still chewing waitress, "Three orders of catfish and hushpuppies please. And three large colas."

"Gotcha. Be right back with your order."

Mandy ran her palm over the top of her head, leaving the short hair looking like a newly cut lawn. She blinked a few times and spoke again. "Smells good in here. I'm starved."

151

Clyde beamed. Laura tapped her fingernails on the table. She had one side of the booth. Clyde was scrunched up next to Mandy on the other side, still with the excuse of holding her up.

The older sister looked around as she rubbed her buttocks, surprised at how sore it was and wondering how that came to be.

Haldol is administered by deep intramuscular injection into the gluteal region.

Laura noted a bright red dot on the inside of Mandy's elbow. As if by osmosis, Mandy rubbed her fingertips over the blue vein in her arm; making it clear she'd also received Haldol intravenously.

Laura's gorge rose. She felt revulsion and guilt over her former jealousy feelings. Those fucking animals shot her up in her arm and her ass. Poor baby. Laura's eyes watered.

Mandy seemed to be coming out of it, somewhat. She was staring at Laura now. "What's going on?"

Laura took a deep breath and explained how she and Clyde had found her at that horrible place. She told her sister everything else, or as much as she knew. Big droplets the size of pumpkin seeds soaked the pink cheeks of the hungry sister. Between sniffles, she proclaimed her gratitude. "Thank you both. Thanks for saving me."

Laura squirmed. The green monster reared again. *Why are family relationships so difficult? How can I care about her so much and then fill with black furious emotions swamping me, burying all that love?*

Ordering popular dishes means less wait time. The food arrived. The steaming dishes were heaped with some of the most delicious food on the planet. Others might not agree; but not at this table. Emotions cooled down, tears dried up and shiny utensils dug in, lifting crispy tasty morsels to open mouths. Conversation all but halted while they dined.

When the plates were emptied, plans were formed. "I don't want to go home."

"Don't worry, Mandy, you're not gonna."

"I have no money and Clyde; they took your totem."

"I know. We think we know who has it."

Mandy scoured her plate, seeking solace in food. Short intake and puff of air. "How's Hannah?"

Laura and Clyde stopped talking. Clyde looked away. Laura shook her head, raised her fist and dropped it.

Mandy's eyes bulged. "What? Tell me."

Laura said gently, "It's just that, she's troubled."

Mandy's volume increased. "Troubled?"

"She's doing good in school. She's a smart kid. She's a natural born leader and has, I can only describe it as 'fans.' Arriona calls it 'Hannah's followers.'"

Now Clyde's face tightened. Then lightning fast, a tiny smile bloomed on his beautiful lips. He thought, That's my girl.

The smug look didn't escape Laura, who continued. "She does have a penchant for lying and keeping secrets."

"What secrets? Why didn't anyone tell me these things?"

"Well Clyde, my mother has been the one responsible for Hannah since you and…" swinging her gaze toward Mandy Rose, "are never around."

Mandy's head dropped, which spoke volumes.

Clyde said, "Let's get to my house where you can get some rest, clear your head and think about making some decisions."

Mandy nodded.

Laura's emotions swung again as she rolled her eyes, looking away toward the other booths.

Laura and Clyde both threw twenties on the table and began wiggling out of the booth to head out of the restaurant.

The waitress was giddy as she added up in her head what her tip would be.

Mandy was slid out also and each held one elbow. The trio traipsed out the door.

The night was humid.

Clyde smiled.

Laura frowned.

Mandy shuddered.

CHAPTER 61

"I'm telling yah Jango, we gotta get those fucken' Voodoo things."

"Who the fuck do you think you're talking to? I make the decisions."

"Yeah, but that crazy cop broad snuffed Chalker."

Jango pinched his chin over and over, not answering, thinking about what Bull just said. Bull wasn't too bright, but this time he might have something. Could be right. "Okay you fat prick, let's go to the club, see if everything's d'accord."

Bull couldn't keep a huge juicy smile from growing on his bulbous lips. He pressed his luck with a jubilant, "Okay, boss." Jango glared at him until Bull's grin swallowed itself whole.

Bull jumped into the Cadillac's driver's seat, followed by Jango who took his time getting into the back seat. Bull turned to look at Jango who was staring out of the window and jumped when Jango yelled, "Go, what're you waiting for?" It was a ten-minute drive to the club.

Jango's mouth dropped open when he spotted the front door of the club ajar. He mumbled, "What the fuck?" Both men moved fast; entered the dark interior of their most secret and valued real estate, their clubhouse. Bull stepped back in deference to let Jango enter first. Jango, with his own safety in mind, shoved the much larger man through the door's opening.

"Holy shit, boss. Holy shit."

They walked around the mound of flesh on the floor. Jango gave it a kick. It stirred. "He ain't dead." Jango, inside now, also saw what was more disturbing. He walked over to a wall and punched it in fury.

He knelt in front of the safe. "Fuck! Fuck! Fuck! It's that God damned bitch cop. Her days are numbered."

Jango stuck his hand into the mostly empty safe and pulled out the remaining totem; the least powerful one that didn't matter for shit. "These fuckers aren't gonna get away with this."

"Yeah, boss. We need that power."

"Shut the fuck up, you moron."

"Awright, but whadda we do now?"

"First we find Mimi. Shoulda capped her little ass a long time ago."

Little did the two sadistic butchers know that Clyde had given Mimi enough money to get on a bus and head to Miami, a long-time dream of hers. He'd also promised to send her more. She trusted him to keep his word. For Clyde, money had become a whole different mindset. No longer poor, he gave it little thought.

"What should we do with Sasquatch here, boss?" The man on the floor was sitting up, both legs spread out in a Vee.

"You shot?"

"I don't think so." His voice a soft growl, low and scratchy.

"I don't see no blood. What happened?"

"It was so fast. I came in here and…"

"Why? Why'd you come in here?"

"Wanted to have a drink."

"A drink?" Jango's face went crimson, his jaw jutted out scraping his teeth.

"Yeah, had my flask." He patted his bulging back pocket.

"Give it to me."

Sasquatch handed the flat silver flask to Jango. Jango unscrewed the top and tilted it into his mouth and gulped the liquid. "Ahhh, so, what the fuck happened?"

"The juju. It was the juju."

"Make sense."

"Honest. She didn't have a gun, just the jujus."

"She? Who she?"

"You know. That broad we took the juju from."

"Which broad? You either make sense or I'll fucking plug you right now myself." Jango had a small pistol out, aiming it at the hapless man who still sat on the floor.

"It was the first chick; no that's wrong. It was the second chick. No, it was the first chick but the second juju. She had both jujus."

"Both?"

"Yeah, it was the one with the long brown hair. She's the one that got away with that other bitch; one… had the sort of shaved head." Bull looked to one side, remembered. "It was like I got struck by thunder. A big noise knocked me cold."

"Holy shit. You mean Camille. I know who that is. I broke her in, spent a whole week with her. She was sweet as candy." Jango licked his lips.

"Yeah, that's who. You passed her around when you was done with her."

"Yeah, yeah. We gotta find both those bitches. We gotta find that little rich bitch. I never even got a taste of that. Okay, first order of the day, get those jujus back, or our whole damn operation will be fucked. Call a search out. I want all three of them, Camille, the rich bitch and the cop." "Boss, there's still one totem in the safe." Looking for points.

"No good, you idiot. No power. A minor juju."

Still trying, Bull put on his bright face and said, "What about the little chick, the one who'll be the priestess. The one called Hannah?"

"Yes, little Hannah. She's almost ready for plucking. Almost twelve years old. Old enough to be snatched and used. I know where she lives. Soon we'll seize her. Yes, capture little Hannah. Grab her and use her."

CHAPTER 62

"Angus, what's happening? You've hardly been home. Did you make any arrests yet?"

"Sophie, honey, yes we did. We have enough proof to know that the man Laura shot who died was part of a ring. They kidnapped children for organ removal."

Sophie's face blanched as she recalled the first time she'd heard these horrors mentioned. The Leprosarium materialized before her mind's eye. She clenched her breast, remembering how her heart had stopped with cold terror not knowing if Hannah was part of that group of children.

Angus saw the fear on her face. "Sophie, stop torturing yourself. Hannah is home now where she belongs."

Sophie tilted her head toward the hallway where Hannah's bedroom was and grasped her throat. The lump formed again as she relived the eerie sounds that had come out of that room. Nobody was in that room but her granddaughter, yet it sounded as though she wasn't alone; that another person's voice sang out with those strange sounding words. Like a chanting. Almost… no not almost, definitely evil. Sophie wanted a drink. Her eyes glossed over with wanting, craving, yearning. Maybe just one gin and tonic. Just one.

Angus watched as Sophie lost focus and stared off into another dimension that she couldn't share with him. He moved closer to her and rubbed her back. He could barely feel her spine. All the fat she'd lost had returned. He knew this troubled her.

Sophie shook her head to clear away the cobwebs. "Do you know yet where my daughters are?" There was a hint of accusation in the statement.

"No, I'm sorry we don't." Angus emphasized the word "we." And continued. "The police in NOLA are looking for Laura. They've put out an APB. You know, they'll have to arrest her for killing that man and shooting the woman."

"What will happen to her?"

"When we get the whole story, it's likely she'll eventually be released; maybe a charge for carrying a pistol. Her government issue wasn't in her possession as you know."

Sophie sat down heavily into a dining room chair that squeaked in protest. Her face scrunched up in disgust at herself.

The phone rang.

Sophie leapt off the chair, knocking it to the floor, and flew to the instrument. "Hello."

"Mama?"

"Yes, oh my God, Laura. Where are you? How are you? Are you okay?"

Angus strode over to his wife, leaning his ear toward the handset.

From somewhere in NOLA: "Mama, don't worry, please. I'm with Clyde and we have Mandy."

"Is she okay. Please tell me she's okay."

"Yes, she's fine. We're taking good care of her."

"What's that mean? Why do you have to take care of her? I thought you said she was fine. Where are you?"

"I have to go now, Mama. Please don't worry."

"Laura!"

"I'm hanging up now. I love you." *Click.*

Sophie fell onto the bottom stair and let the phone fall from her hand. Angus squatted down in front of her at the bottom of the huge curved golden staircase. He rubbed her knees and was surprised to find a stray thought poking at his brain. *Why do people think being wealthy means a charmed life?*

He had to ask. "Sophie, did she say where she was?"

Sophie's brow furrowed. She flung angry words at Angus. "Why? You gonna go there and arrest her?"

"No dear, I'm not. But sooner or later that will happen, and she'll have to face being charged with her crimes."

Hannah stood straight as an arrow in the archway, listening. Her hands were folded and leaned on her slender groin. "Gramma Sophie."

Sophie's head jerked up and she repeated the oft-expressed phrase, "Hannah, please just call me Gramma."

Hannah, in a consolatory mood, acquiesced. "Gramma, did Auntie Laura find my father?" Then she twisted her mouth as though these words were more difficult to speak. "And my mother?"

"Yes, honey. They're both in the city."

Hannah tapped her foot. "Are they coming here?"

"Not yet, but soon."

Hannah wanted time alone.

She left to go back to her room. Sophie put her elbows on her knees and held her head up. She said, "Angus, did you hide that news clipping to keep me from reading it?"

Angus's turn to react. "Oh Sophie, I'm sure it doesn't mean anything. It's a small part of the case that's not really connected anymore."

"No Angus, I'm not really sure about that. It happened in the same town in New Jersey where Hannah lived for a while. Valeria was the maid in George and Martha Trenton's house."

Angus waited for Sophie to finish her thoughts.

"I met her when I first found Hannah that day. She was very strict with Hannah, almost cruel. The Trentons had named Hannah, Isabella, and that woman acted like Hannah was her property. And now she's dead. Cardiac infarction. Way too young to have a heart attack."

"Just a coincidence, honey, nothing ominous. Not sure why you believe otherwise."

Sophie peered down the hallway where only moments ago Hannah had slipped and disappeared into her room, where she spent most of her time. Sophie covered her eyes with both hands and mumbled, "Yeah, just a coincidence."

CHAPTER 63

"Mandy, are you feeling good enough to answer some things?" Clyde's tongue had returned to almost normal size and his speech was free of any lisping. This pleased him.

Mandy Rose opened her eyes wide to observe the man she still craved; the father of her daughter. "Yes. I feel very relaxed. My head doesn't hurt. My thoughts aren't jumbled." She raised and lowered her shoulders to give an okay signal.

Clyde dipped his head to one side and slitted his eyes to emphasize the importance of the upcoming conversation. Mandy wiggled her butt in closer to him and listened with a serious look on her face.

"What's the story on that Camille? You trust her, right?"

Mandy blew air out through puffed lips. "I don't know. Not sure. She seemed okay." Mandy blushed a bit, remembering the masturbation and climax. Clyde seemed oblivious. "Clyde, she said they stole her juju too. That's why we both ended up in that awful place."

"Do you think she knows where those creeps keep the amulets?"

"She might. She's been in their grips for a long time."

"This is important now, Mandy. Do you think she was aware of how powerful my gris-gris was?"

"Yeah, Clyde. Pretty sure she was."

Clyde stomped his foot. "Shit."

Laura's back stiffened. She pushed forward to be included in this exchange. "The Watcher" was sending out red clouds with black swirls, thick enough for Laura to see a nonofficial reality appear in their center. She stated with force, "We have to find her before she goes for those amulets. Do you think she'll go to your house."

"Shit, shit, shit." Clyde's face turned to grayish stone; his heart pounded loud enough for them all to almost hear. "We have to go there."

Mandy's face paled. "What about Hannah?"

Clyde swallowed, a great gulping sound. "They'll be after her too. They must know Hannah is the rightful heir to my grandfather's gris-gris. She's at the center of all of this."

Mandy's mouth opened. "Do you think she knows this?"

Clyde dropped to his knees in supplication. "Oh dear Mama Marie, sweet and holy Mama Marie, please hear my plea." Clyde touched his heart from habit, wishing he could feel the familiar shape in his breast pocket. He grabbed a hand from each sister's lap and held the skinny white fingers in his strong brown ones and in a soft otherworldly voice crooned, "Hannah will be touched by all that's happening. She's the chosen one. She's approaching puberty." Then he stopped. His eyes grew large; a raw fresh green color. "Nooo, she's already there… the correct age. We have no time. We have to get to her."

"What about the gris-gris?"

Clyde put his thumb and forefinger to his forehead and pushed as though he might squeeze out the right answers; the best path to take. "You two go back home and stay with Hannah. Try to make her understand what she's probably already going through. I'll find Camille 'cause I don't trust her. I think I'll also find the amulets. I'm sure she knew where to get them."

Laura and Mandy nodded.

Clyde wasn't sure Camille would go to his house, but he damn well felt she wanted those gris-gris. What he didn't know was how power-hungry the woman was.

Mandy Rose said, "I'm not going home, Clyde, can't face Mama or any of that. Please get me a cab to take me to your house so I can rest. I need to rest."

Clyde smoothed Mandy's back and did as she desired. After he called a cab for her, he called the mansion to tell them to watch over Hannah. Bring in the chauffeur if Angus isn't there. Get the gun in the liquor cabinet. Or better still, maybe even take Hannah out of the house.

He made the call. He expected to be the one with dire news and instructions about the dangers to Hannah. He was cut off. "Oh Clyde, I'm so glad to hear from you. I'm so worried about Hannah. I'm afraid she may run away. We believe she already did this before but came back."

Clyde tried soothing words to placate Sophie. Still in his thoughts he was in misery. She was just a little girl, but what might happen to her, and what was she capable of?

CHAPTER 64

Camille hungered for power. She wanted the total power bestowed on the High Priestess. She craved it with a vengeance. She'd get that title if she had the gris-gris stolen from Mandy Rose. That stupid bitch. The girl was weak, pathetic. Hard to imagine how she ever got possession of the most powerful gris-gris in existence. 'Cause of Clyde of course. He knew what it meant. *Even those barbarians who captured me and took my anemic gris-gris knew what could be accomplished with the juju inherited by Clyde.* That totem could lead them to the children they needed to get wealthy. Kids who weren't watched and cared about; kids who wouldn't be missed. Mostly throw-away kids. The organs in their little bodies might as well be made of fourteen carat gold. *There's no limit on what this gris-gris I now own can accomplish. It's capable of everything. There are no limits.*

Camille sniffed. A slight musky odor. No, it smelled like a smudge. Her nostrils flared. She said aloud in a soft tone, "White sage?" A sensation of heat in her right pocket. Light drifting out. Now it glowed. Christ, the material was smoking. What to do. What to do.

A grasping fear tightened her throat. She had to act. Reaching into her left pocket, Camille yanked out her old familiar totem. Useless damn thing. Swinging her hand over to the other pocket, she pushed knuckle first deeper to the bottom, trying to stuff the piece of shit gris-gris in on top of the smoldering gris-gris. A high-pitched whistle careened around her head with great swirls, making her hair fly in circles with the electro-magnetic energy.

She sat down on the curb; not sure what to do. Her knees quivered. She had a tiger by the tail, an unknown otherness with no precedent. A roiling vacuum filled her chest, threatening her heart with extinction. She had to act. On instinct she pulled out both totems. Together they trembled in her hands. Her eyes bulged. A breathy sound huffed and puffed into the night air.

"Huh, huh, huh, huh. Hannnaahhhh. Hannnaahhhh. Hannnaahhhh."

The young woman's body quaked. Her mouth slid down, pouring out a steady stream of drool that darkened the front of her shirt. Her lips hardened, the increased weight becoming little wooden logs. Camille's thighs compressed until she screamed in anguish. She couldn't lift them. Steel girders.

She bellowed, "Stop, stop, stop. Please stop. What do you want?"

Again the huffing whispers. "Hannnaahhhh. Hannnaahhhh. Hannnaahhhh."

"Stop. I'll take you to her."

Droplets from an invisible realm gushed down to her blistering thighs; mountains of sulfur scented steam curled upward. Camille's brain reached into much forgotten Christian beliefs and sinister words formed. Fire and brimstone. Hell fire. Hell.

Camille strained to make sense of it all. She was not going to the mansion where that little girl lived. Instead, brain patterns were instructing her to go to the father's house. Go to Clyde's. Right now. Clyde's.

CHAPTER 65

Sophie settled into her favorite armchair and sipped lemonade from a tall frosty glass. Angus's report on the progress of the organ trafficking was encouraging. The two teenage boys outdid themselves being helpful.

Detective Sloane'd used his influence to impress internal affairs in the investigation of Laura; making a plea on her behalf. There were enough witnesses to the first shooting that made any conclusion other than self-defense almost impossible.

The shooting at the Voodoo building turned up enough evidence for proof of a connection to the organ trafficking trade to show that activities were being practiced from that site. Still sketchy was how Voodoo was used to aid these crimes. Sophie figured Clyde might be helpful in that area.

A loud noise near the front door. The clamor roused her out of her musings.

The deep voice was easily recognized. Sophie pushed herself out of the soft chair and exclaimed, "Clyde! Oh my God, Clyde!"

The entering man and woman bolted over to where Sophie stood and was now holding her hand to her chest, making soft moist coughing sounds.

"Mama, are you all right?"

"Oh Laura, I'm so glad to see you. Yes, I'm okay." She reached into her pocket and pulled out a bright red canister she shook several time then pushed into her mouth. *Whoosh, whoosh.* Sophie inhaled the albuterol sulfate, which she now always kept on her person. It worked. Her face seemed to melt into a more relaxed state. Laura's pupils dilated as her mother's bronchial tubes spread open and smoothed out.

Sophie's arm dropped to her side; the red cannister still in her fist. "Where's Mandy Rose?" "She's headed to my house, maybe already there. She wanted to rest up alone before she came back home." Clyde's face stayed neutral.

"Is she okay? Rest up from what?"

Laura picked up on the explanation here. As she patted her mother's shoulder, she said in an almost hypnotic voice designed to calm and console, "She had a mild incident, but she's much better now."

Sophie envisioned Mandy's beautiful hair that her daughter had sheared off and tried to picture this Mandy Rose as being "much better now." Sophie had those long brown strands, tied in the middle with a white velvet ribbon, tucked away in a jewelry box amidst gold rings and bracelets.

Would her older daughter ever be "much better now?" A wave of hatred started in her gut and moved to her throat as she once again felt the need to throw up the knowledge of the abuse that Harold had inflicted on a young Mandy Rose. Her own father! Sophie was glad Harold was dead. She hoped he burned in Hell.

"Mama, are you okay?"

"Yes, fine."

"We came here to see Hannah."

"Why? Why now? What's wrong? What aren't you telling me?"

"Don't worry about that now. Is she in her room?"

A small high-pitched voice that now joined the unfolding drama proclaimed, "She's gone!"

"What do you mean, Arriona? Gone where?"

The child had the eyes and demeaner of a much older person. She set her features in the manner of someone not prone to panic but imparting necessary information. "I don't know how long ago she left." Pause. "But she took her doll."

Laura bent over at the waist; balled fists to her sides. "What doll?"

Clyde stepped closer to the little girl. His mouth fell open as though he could catch more of the answer when it came.

"She has a doll that she made?"

Clyde questioned, "Does she talk to it?"

Arriona took a second, then, "Yes, all the time."

Clyde's face went closer. "What else?"

Arriona looked to her side as though she didn't expect to be believed, uttered nothing.

Clyde tried again. "What else, Arriona?"

Arriona said, "Um."

"It's okay honey, just tell me whatever you know. Don't be afraid."

More quietly, Arriona said, "Um, I hear a different voice sometimes."

Clyde pushed on, keeping his voice soft to match Arriona's. "How different? What do you mean?"

"Uh, different, like it's not Hannah."

Sophie's head drifted left and right as she admitted to herself she'd also heard that *different* voice.

"The different voice Arriona, can you describe it?"

Arriona's eyes brimmed with moisture, her face frozen.

"It's okay sweetheart, just tell me what this other-sounding voice was like."

Arriona trusted Clyde. She smoothed down the yoke of her cocoa-colored dress and spoke. "It's like a man. It's deep and scary. It's like a creepy ghost man." Arriona took a step back as her balance teetered. Her leather shoes made a single tap sound.

Nobody said anything.

Clyde walked over to the trembling child and put both arms around her. "Thank you, honey. You did good."

"Yeah, but..." her eyes went wild, the whites showing like a frightened filly.

Clyde patted her back. "What's the matter?"

"But, but, I'm afraid of Hannah. Lots of the kids at school are afraid of Hannah too. She'll be mad at me for telling."

Clyde now smoothed the child's back with tender strokes and reassured her she was not in any danger and was safe.

Clyde looked up from Arriona to Laura and jutted his chin toward the door they'd come through mere moments ago.

Sophie saw the act. "Are you leaving?"

"Yes, we're going to my house. That's where Mandy Rose should be resting." He waited a few seconds. "And probably where Hannah is headed."

Laura nodded, hugged Arriona and kissed her mother goodbye.

Once they'd gone out and the car was heard roaring off, Sophie opened her arms wide. Arriona flew into them. Talking in muffled tones against Sophie's breast, she said, "I'm scared of Hannah, Gramma Sophie. I feel so bad about that."

Sophie cleared her throat and responded, "I understand honey," and she added, "I'm also afraid. Not just of her but *for* Hannah."

The two stood consoling each other as darkness settled around the mansion; a heavy shroud descending as voices quietened.

CHAPTER 66

Hannah sat on the bus headed to her father's house. The rolling tires spun out a humming sound. The continuous drone merged with her brain's pattern. She felt herself deepening and lowering into a cavern of otherness. In an altered state, she shifted her gaze from one passenger to the next, then to another. The buzzing rumble blotted out all human voices until all that remained was the pulsing sound of a million bees. Her vision was smudged with a delicate veil as her awareness became crystal clear; a raindrop glistening.

Her half lidded eyes surveilled the passengers, halting with each new face. She felt their life story. Not the everyday details, a more fully comprehensive story; their story. She knew their worldview in vivid detail. She knew *them*. Not just this present lifetime where they were focused but all their lifetimes. She was inside their very essence. Inside their soul.

The experience exhilarated her as she drifted from person to person. Again, their entire comprehension of all that existed within their lives; on all their journeys, both physical and non-physical, in every universe and every dimension.

Their "Weltanschauung."

Hannah felt at home. Power was hers. Freedom was hers. Her awareness expanded out to galaxies both physical and non-physical, then her consciousness contracted to a single dot that was her. She went in and out and felt no fear.

The bus rumbled to a stop. She looked up as though awakening from another world.

She stood and scuffled along the aisle to the door that opened, making a wretched screech when the driver pushed on the lever by the steering wheel. She ambled down the metal stairs that let her, the only passenger, out onto a road that was little more than a wide dirt path. This road that traveled past the vintage houses still standing after decades of use. Small houses, some of which were upgrades from the shacks that sheltered the negro slaves. A roof over the heads of African Americans who'd spent their mostly short-lived existences crammed together into tiny places, creating the illusion of freedom from the tyranny they suffered under.

Hannah's face drew down as she tapped into her father's early childhood. A black screen in her mind's eye showed a well-lit hole as she viewed him in his raggedy gray pants and scuffed brown shoes, shoes that tortured his growing feet. The eyes, oh the eyes, way too old for a nine-year-old boy. She glimpsed his grandpa, her great-grandpa, as he was led to the waving noose that hung from the gnarly branch of the poplar tree. Grandpa's eyes looked skyward; fixed toward a world not physical. His worn boots still laced around his bony ankles.

Little Clyde again. The boy's heart jerked, threatening his youthful chest. The unruly brutes cried out, "Find a small branch. Hang the little nigger too."

Then the white lady in the big white hat came to his rescue, her eyes wide with outrage. "Leave him alone. He's just a boy."

"Yeah, but he'll turn into a full-grown black buck who'll rape our women."

Her back stiffened and she leaned toward the crazed rednecks. "Leave him alone I said."

The boy didn't know why but could tell she had *say* in the matter. The pasty-faced brute whose dirty shirt didn't stay buttoned on his bloated belly dropped the still unformed rope, earmarked for hanging an unusually small lynch victim, his face contorted with rage at having his entertainment curtailed.

Hannah watched as a movie reel played out for her; the only audience.

The boy's eyes brimmed with tears as his beloved granddaddy got hauled up by the neck while a throng of white men, young and old, yelled obscenities and cheered.

"String 'em up."

Little Clyde watched and learned to hate. But in his pocket was his salvation.

The gris-gris that'd been passed decades ago to his granddaddy was now his. It awaited a female to be born into the family to take full possession of its ginormous power; its legacy of unparalleled greatness.

Hannah's vision cleared as she lowered herself down the metal steps of the bus. She was aware that *time* as she knew it had stopped while she observed all she'd just seen.

The tiny kiosk was the only place cabs stopped to pick people up, seldom to drop people off. The bus driver opened his mouth to voice concerns about her destination but thought better of it, just slammed the folding door shut after her.

Hannah knew where she was going. She had a mission. Her whole body screamed for consummation.

Her little jaw jutted out. Her shoulders squared as she grew an inch taller, or so it seemed. She was ready.

CHAPTER 67

I need to sleep. Sleep will help me heal. Maybe too much has happened here to relax and recover. Flashes too horrific to bring in clearly crashed into Mandy Rose's mind; pictures, awful pictures. Felix… on top of her, gouging her thighs with his fat dirty fingernails. She heard herself making small animal whimpering sounds. She heard Felix grunting, forming the words "little girl" in his violent attack on her impaled body. The rapist unaware of the buried putrid memories associated with those two little words from daddy dearest. Good too because it unleashed power she didn't dream she possessed as she threw him over, shackled as he was by his lowered pants, making him weak as a trussed hog. Fast on her feet, she'd made headway, clamored out the small open bedroom window only she could fit through and escaped. Running, running, lungs on fire while the brute aimed his pistol at her, firing a barrage of bullets that kept missing their mark. She remembered it all. Then, the miracle. Bertie's green Porsche. This thought soothed her, though sweat drenched the sheets she lay on, releasing long harbored mildew odors. Her mind blanked out for several minutes then fired up again with recent horrors. She yearned for peace. Would she ever be at peace?

She felt a deep need for a shower but was so tired it seemed comparable to lifting her T-Bird. The dark thoughts swirled, loaded with toxins. Yes, the mental hospital. Lying there, unable to move, too drugged to cry out, she'd been molested. Yes, those two creeps had exposed her and buried their tongues inside her. She felt sick to her stomach. She felt dirty. Was that when she'd fainted? She'd heard voices then. Yes, that's when she was rescued. Yes, thank God. Clyde and Laura got her out of there. How did they know to do that?

Her head pounded and ached. She wanted fresh air. Was she strong enough to get up on her own and open the window? The same window she'd squeezed through when she fled for her life, barely escaping that

170

piece of shit rapist, Felix. She shook her head to dislodge these black memories.

She pushed to a sitting position then swung her legs over the side of the bed. The sheets were pulled up, exposing a striped mattress with rust-colored stains. She averted her eyes.

Yes, the window faced her. A wave of light-headedness and nausea threatened to keep her in place on the fetid bed. Deep breaths. In through the nose for a count of seven, hold for four, then out through pursed lips counting to eight. Do it again. The room came into view with sharper edges.

She faced the window. Her bare feet touched the floor that used to be so familiar. Yes, this was where Hannah was conceived.

Hannah, oh Hannah. *I've been so neglectful.* She shook her head to purge those thoughts, resolved for the hundredth time to do better.

Two labored steps and her hands reached for the bars on the window, disturbing some peeling paint chips. Still weak, she heard a humph sound. The window moved. It scraped upward. The air was glorious. She bent a little, placed her face into the slight breeze, taking in the intimate smells of the native trees and shrubs. The sweet scent was almost too heady for her still queasy stomach. She tried to identify the species. Verbena? Jasmine? But, oh so rejuvenating. She thrilled to the feeling of energy returning, her legs regaining strength.

Then her heart stopped.

Stopped like a broken clock whose gears wouldn't mesh. A sharper noise.

"Who's there?"

No answer, but the scuffling of approaching feet. Again, "Who's there? Who is it? Clyde? Laura?" Again, no answer.

Mandy Rose was stricken; her mouth went dry, and she looked around for something to use as a weapon.

Feeling strong now, she grabbed an old metal shower curtain rod that stood in the corner. Her mind sharp, she deduced that whoever had invaded her space had nothing good in mind. She took up a crouched position behind the flimsy bedroom door and raised the heavy pole in readiness. Footsteps coming closer.

The door creaked slowly open. Someone entered. Mandy Rose, convinced she was in danger facing a prowler, up to no good, robbery or worse, swung the pole down… hard.

All her strength went into that single bludgeoning. Before she determined who the intruder was, she clubbed the invader again. *Bam.* Her vision blurred. Again. *Bam.* A solid hit, on the unwelcome visitor's head.

There was blood on the silver pole. The body sank, crumpled, legs splayed and long beige hair turning crimson by inches.

Mandy dropped to her knees, letting the shower rod clatter onto the tile floor.

"Oh my God. What've I done? Camille!"

Mandy felt the young woman's neck for a pulse. There, but very weak. A feeble sound that seemed erratic, almost a flutter.

Mandy checked the bedside table where a telephone sat caked with dust and undoubtedly out of order for many months. She sat down flat on the floor.

She could do nothing except wait for Laura and Clyde to come back to check on her. She had no tears left in her. The breeze from the window now chilled her.

A movement caught her eye. The probably dying young woman's hand uncurled. Mandy's head snapped around and watched, spellbound as the fingers dropped open exposing two totems.

One, a strange cloth type of juju with some beige jute string tied around it and some lavender sparkles with areas that were missing. It appeared wrinkled.

But the other. *Oh my God*, the other. Clyde's gris-gris.

Mandy held her breath as she slipped her hand under the totem and lifted it reverently. Clyde's gris-gris, back in her possession. She scrunched it into her front pocket, switching her attention to the now graying face of Camille. The woman's jaw had gone slack and her eyes now stared vacantly at the ceiling. This was bad. She shook her head. What had she done? And why did Camille have Clyde's gris-gris?

CHAPTER 68

"Sophie, are you okay?"

Cassy stood behind Arriona, dropping her long arms around her daughter in a hug that wrapped all the way to both sides of her slim and perfect child. Arriona twisted her neck to look up at her mother, accustomed to such shows of affection but changing how she felt about it. She was getting older and was self-conscious; not sure if it was cool. "Oh, Ma!"

Cassy tightened her embrace for a second then released her daughter.

Sophie still hadn't answered. She watched the mother and daughter and yearned for the same open lovingness with Hannah but doubted it would ever happen. "I'm fine, Cassy. I'm thinking we should call Angus, also thinking we should go to Clyde's."

Cassy nodded. Her features tightened into a different expression; brows coming together and lips revealing the tip of a very pink tongue. "Is Almadine still here?" Cassy questioned.

"Yes, she's still here. I'll make sure she can stay with Arriona. We'll meet Angus at Clyde's."

Arriona protested. "I wanna go too."

Sophie moved closer to the *almost teenager* and took both her hands. "Arriona, we're not sure what to expect there. You know we're concerned about Hannah's state of mind."

Arriona twisted her mouth then said, "I know more than you do."

"What do you know? You have to tell us."

"She warned me not to tell you stuff."

Sophie glanced at Cassy over Arriona's head. Arriona was tapping her foot and closed her mouth into a slim purple line. "Arriona, please tell us what you know."

The two women waited.

"Please tell us." The young girl tilted her head then reluctantly whispered, "Okay… only you won't believe me."

Sophie said in an even voice, "Yes, we will believe you."

Arriona licked her lips and uttered, "I already told you some stuff. Hannah has two voices. I hear two people when I know she's alone."

Sophie leaned back into the table and grasped it behind her buttocks. "Oh God, child. I told you, I believe you. I've heard it also. I didn't want to admit it to myself. I've been denying what I know I've heard with my own ears. What else do you know?"

"Hannah goes out at night." Arriona chewed her cheek. She hated being a tattletale. She stays out for hours and comes back home. Everyone is sleeping, but I hear her."

"Okay, honey. You did the right thing telling us. We want to help Hannah. Thank you."

Arriona felt relieved, a heavy burden lifted from her slender shoulders.

Sophie called out to the kitchen, "Almadine."

Their maid entered the room, drying her hands on a green terry cloth dishtowel. Eyes wide, she took in the stricken faces of the women and the sloped posture of the girl. "What's the matter? What's going on?"

"Can you stay here this evening with Arry?"

"Yes'm, I sure can. She can help me make some beignets. I wasn't going out anyway, planned to bake dis evening."

Sophie's face smoothed out as she walked briskly over to the telephone. Angus needed to meet them at Clyde's.

As she reached her hand out to pick up the receiver the phone rang. "Hello."

"Sophie, it's me. I have news."

"What Angus, what news?" Sophie stiffened her back, waiting for more trouble. Angus let the silence sit for half a minute, then said without preamble, "Felix Guidry is dead."

Sophie gasped. The man who'd kidnapped Hannah was dead. She backed into the staircase, letting herself drop down to sit on the lower step. The receiver dangled from her hand as she tried to consume and process this information. Recovered sufficiently to speak, she said, "How? How did he die? Was it murder like Harry? Did someone murder him?" She knew that prisoners who hurt children were pariahs and often met with disaster, even death.

"No Sophie. He wasn't murdered. The story says he was in the mess hall. There was no foul play. He was tipping a bowl of lentils up to his mouth and slurping the lumpy liquid when he started choking. He grabbed his chest, dropped the bowl and keeled over into his bread dish."

"Oh my God, that's so strange."

"Yeah, he was dead before anyone had a chance to do anything to save him. What was really weird was about half of the prisoners started clapping. And truth be known, no one tried to give him any help. By the time the guards got to his body, all that was left to do was carry him out of the cafeteria. He was a big guy. It took three guards to move him."

"Oh," was all Sophie said.

"Sophie honey, try not to let this bother you. I'll be home later. We'll have dinner together tonight. I have to go now. Love you." And the phone's dial tone was screaming in Sophie's ear.

Sophie felt like she was coming out of a cloud. It seemed like the end of something. But it also felt like another shoe had to drop.

Arriona watched all this, felt left out; knew she'd been kept in the dark. She looked forward to time alone with Almadine.

The maid, aware that something ominous had happened, chirped, "Let's get into the kitchen, honey. We have to clear a spot for rolling out the dough for our beignets."

Arriona let the sides of her lips curl up as she followed Almadine out of the room.

Cassy eyeballed Sophie and said, "Tell me about it in the car. Let's get going."

Sophie was proud of herself. Her asthma hadn't kicked up. Maybe good news wasn't stressful for her lungs.

As soon as the duo were in the car and the doors slammed shut, Sophie yelped. "Oh, shit!"

Cassy turned to her seatmate. "What?" She'd never heard Sophie swear before.

"I forgot to tell Angus to meet us at Clyde's"

"Don't worry, we have the Rover; you can call him right back."

Cassy pulled the bulky phone out of her purse and handed it to Sophie. "You know how to use that, don't you?"

Sophie was already pushing buttons.

CHAPTER 69

Clyde's little house would soon be bursting with people.

Camille wasn't moving. Still as a concrete statue. Lying in the same position where she'd fallen on the bedroom floor. Mandy put two fingers to the woman's neck and let out a tiny gasp. The pulse wasn't just weak. There was no pulse. She put her ear to Camille's chest. Silence. No telephone to call for help; too late anyway. She held her head in her hands and closed her eyes, imagining a dead and buried Camille and herself in prison for murder.

Pop! Her eyes sprang open, her vision clear. She dropped her hands to the floor to guide herself into a kneeling position. The air was alive. Rippling like a tide on a faraway beach. She closed her eyes and waited. Her spinning brain stopped. She pushed herself to her feet, then held on to the door jamb till she felt calm and stable. She felt almost like herself.

Mandy hoped "the door" would be open. The door to the special room. Feeling stronger, she still wasn't sure she could batter the door to Clyde's Voodoo shrine open.

Running her fingertips along the wall in the short hallway, she made her way to Clyde's private enclosed shrine. The door to the room wasn't locked. A strange matter of fact, it was ajar. Odd.

She patted the gris-gris in her pocket, drawing strength from its presence. She entered the room.

Once inside, all manner of phenomena started up. She held her hand to her throat as candles lit of their own accord. The foot-high statue of the Virgin Mother began to shimmer with a golden nimbus that glowed more than six inches around Jesus's mother's bowed head. Numerous ruby-colored stones and velvet cloths grew rich in technicolor pigment, an artist's paradise.

Mandy lowered herself to a marble stool encrusted on all sides with more rubies. She took Clyde's gris-gris from her pocket and held it out on her outstretched palm facing the ceiling. Words began to form. The letters materialized from a silvery steam. They pulsed and sparkled.

"Relay the Force Pattern as a Source of Tension…"

Mandy's whole body relaxed. She was breathing in and out easily. Peace was hers. But for how long?

The only light in the tiny, crowded room came from the big red block letters. Her arms and hands were bathed in crimson. She knew all would be ending soon. She didn't know how. She didn't know what.

She was so very tired.

Soon, it will all be over.

Tears streamed down her upturned face; the droplets lit up and rosy colored; yes, from the reflected glow of the red letters. Something big was ready to burst, something that would change everything. One word slipped from between her lips: "Soon."

CHAPTER 70

Clyde and Laura looked at each other with stricken faces. Both felt a building urgency about to explode.

Laura's "Watcher" …on high alert. "The Watcher" screamed in actual words, the audio version of its usual telepathic method. It yelled, "Relay the Force Pattern as a Source of Tension…"

Laura grabbed Clyde's shoulders, her hands like steel clamps. "We have to get there before Hannah does."

Clyde's green eyes bulged, pregnant emeralds. Sweat trickled down his back and glistened his forehead. "Yes, Laura. Let's move."

No time to waste, the pair jumped into a white sports car that some jackass, lucky for them, had left the keys hanging out of the ignition. A half dollar size orange basketball was attached to the chain.

Clyde drove, and Laura kept her foot on an invisible gas pedal. The macadam was swallowed whole as they roared down the ill-paved roads leading to Clyde's. Laura's light body weight kept her lifting in the air while Clyde clung to the steering wheel for purchase.

Darkness shrouded the street as the first of the broken down four-room shacks appeared. Little light came from most of the sad homes. An occasional small window yellow with artificial low wattage light bulbs gleamed a dim path through the dark and dreary road. Black limbed live oak trees spread their grasping branches with obnoxious abandon.

Cassy and Sophie were shocked when the white sports car zoomed past them on the little-traveled road. Neither recognized the vehicle.

Sophie's head swiveled in the direction of the driver's seat and bellowed, "Oh my God. That's Clyde driving that car."

"You broke my ear drums. Are you sure?"

"Yes, I'm sure. Someone else was with him. Someone smaller."

Cassy jammed more weight on the pedal her foot was attached to, and they closed the distance between the Jag and the white car.

178

Now they were sure. Clyde and someone else were heading to Clyde's too.

CHAPTER 71

The Rover on Sophie's lap jangled its strange announcement of an incoming call. Cassy looked down at the red light, said, "Answer it."

Sophie picked up the cop phone and said, loud enough to be heard over the engine noise, "Hello?"

"Is that you, Sophie?"

"Yes… Angus?"

"Yes, listen to me. Something's going on. There've been two reports of disasters. Explosions. One at that house where the traffickers were keeping the kids. We're planning a sting at that very place tonight. It was full of those bastards trying to make a getaway. They refused to leave behind any identifying evidence, porn videos, bondage toys or sadistic trade tools. The whole place blew up. And," Angus took a deep breath, "another house full of these creeps, some from other countries, also… *kaboom*. It's crazy. Almost like the universe is taking charge and doing our job. At this point we have no clue as to the cause of either of these explosions. There'll be plenty of bodies to collect. I should head over there, even though there's nothing left to do but collect the bodies."

Sophie sat very still, not answering. She had to follow her instincts. A quick decision was made.

"Sophie?"

She managed a soft, "Yes, Angus. I'm here."

"Sophie, what are you thinking?"

Sophie was quick to answer, "I'm not thinking. I'm demanding. Get over to Clyde's. Right now." Rather than wait and be questioned about her powerful command, she hung up. The Rover sat there on her lap, still warm.

"Step on it, Cassy." No need to repeat… the Jag picked up speed with a burst of power befitting the well-equipped piece of automotive machinery.

The pilfered white sports car and Sophie's silver Jag both aimed for the tiny front yard that offered little parking space. Breaks screeched.

All four of the rushing rescuers had their ears deafened by raging sirens. Louder and louder as two squad cars careened into the already packed patch of dirt.

What no one'd noticed; the small figure on the side of the house, casting a shadow three times the length of it. The tiny figure didn't move, just swayed a bit from side to side. One slender arm raised up as though to make an umbrella to cover the whole of Clyde Boudreaux's little house.

Inside the house, Camille lay getting colder and colder on the hard floor. Terrified, Mandy Rose heard all the commotion. Her hands shook violently. She was spellbound at what the gris-gris was doing. It left her palm, lifted, and of its own accord headed straight up. It was caterwauling the words somehow, repeating those from the ceiling in the room where the Voodoo altar resided. "Relay the Force Pattern as a Source of Tension…" The sound of Banshees filled the air. Mandy Rose was stricken dumb, frozen, unable to move. The haunting message seemed to implant itself in her head rather than hearing it with her ears. It lived in her brain.

Outside, the child priestess kept her arm raised. Her face, a perfect mask of tranquility. Her features were smooth, youthful but newly chiseled with the maturity befitting an aged queen. She began to chant in an unholy melody…" Relay the Force Pattern as a Source of Tension…"

Ambulance sirens wound down and the square vehicles pulled up, unable to get too near the crowded space around the house. Back doors to both ambulances were flung open by white suited paramedics.

Sophie screamed, "Mandy Rose, Mandy, please answer. Are you in there?" The fire had begun with a tiny spark in Clyde's Voodoo room and now had turned into a conflagration of mammoth proportions. No normal fire ever spread this fast.

Smoke poured out the front door. A figure appeared in the window on the face of the little house. A slight figure with no indication of gender. The head was round. The shoulders slender. The arms began waving left and right, left and right. "Help… help."

"Oh my God, it's Mandy."

The men in black and yellow fireproof suits had jumped down from a bright red truck outfitted with a hose connected to a tankard of water.

They were getting ready to douse the house being consumed by fire. The fireman in charge bellowed, "This fire is crazy!"

Sophie ran up to the big man and pounded him on the chest. "Go in there. Get my daughter. My daughter's in the house."

The man looked down at the top of Sophie's blonde head and said, "Sorry ma'am, too dangerous to go in there now. That house is about to cave in."

Clyde also saw the figure in the window of what used to be his living room. He heard the dire exchange between Sophie and the fire fighter.

He headed around to the back of the house where the broken-down porch sat. He passed Hannah on the side of the house. She looked at him. Her green eyes, golden and shiny, cat eyes glowing with sentience. She switched her attention and looked skyward. There was an unmistakable whirring sound disturbing the air.

Clyde had to get to Mandy Rose. He couldn't do anything about Hannah who appeared to be in no danger.

Through the porch and past the kitchen where he'd poisoned Bertie, then into the living room where Felix had shot him, left him for dead. He saw Mandy Rose standing there quaking in front of the window that was bright yellow with reflected light from the fire. The smoke billowed and turned the inside of the house dark gray. The gray and yellow colors spelled doom for him and for Mandy Rose unless he moved fast. The fire was blocking the front door. Opening it would create a back draft and the flames would be insurmountable.

He yelled, "Mandy." She stood there shaking, not hearing him above the roar of the fire. He bolted to her, his long legs getting him there in four leaps. He grabbed her, lifted her in his arms and swung around to go back out the way he'd come in.

Bounding across the floor; scorching heat to the bottom of his shoes, he lit out the back way and stopped when something like a giant bird descended into the side yard where he'd last seen Hannah.

He hugged Mandy to his chest and watched, transfixed.

The bird was a helicopter, hovering low enough for Clyde to see who was in there. It floated lower. The passenger door of the tiny cockpit held a child-size figure. The long flowing white hair was painfully familiar. The chopper hesitated above the girl.

The High Priestess let her hair flow out the door of the whirly bird. Now he saw that inside the loose locks was a braid. A thick white braid.

Mambo tilted her head to let the braid drop in a straight line. It must've weighed fifty pounds.

Fascinated, he was unable to do anything as his body was now paralyzed to the spot. He watched. The braid continued its descent, stiff as a steel girder.

The girl stopped pointing at the house, twisted toward the chopper and the High Priestess who smiled at her. Without hesitation, she bent and straightened her arms, elbows out as two small hands grabbed onto the braid, high enough to get a solid grip.

She lifted her legs, crooked knees, hanging in mid-air, hair flying, she turned to look at Clyde and Mandy Rose.

The chopper paused long enough for her to deliver her message.

In an act of miracle proportions, she spoke and could be heard above the raucous din of the fire, the sirens, the screams and shouts. But, no, not true. The words were not audible. It was a form of telepathy. Hannah's lips weren't moving. They were smiling. Her eyes were shiny and bright green. Two traffic lights, beaming down on them.

"Did you not know dear mother and father, I had to be about the business of being Queen Mother. I gave the bad guys what they deserved. Not all as there will always be more. I must leave you now to be with Mambo. She has much to teach me. I love you both." Then she went hand over hand as she climbed the white braid and disappeared into the big noisy bird. A bony long-fingered hand came around her back and welcomed her. The ancient Priestess bowed her head to the little girl's forehead, touching it with her own.

The gris-gris stalled aloft, pulsing, waiting with a phosphorescent glow until the child was inside, then glided with the speed of a 1920's silent film, inexplicably attached to the middle of Hannah's back. The long white fingers of Mambo Marie covered the gris-gris, which continued to glow a bright green between the slender digits.

Sophie watched, not sure if she saw what she thought she saw.

Cassy put her arm around Sophie, and they walked toward Clyde who still carried Mandy Rose in his arms, hugging her close to his heart.

A huge crashing sound erupted as the house, at an impossible speed, crumbled into a pile of gray ashes. Billows of smoke floated skyward, showing tiny particulates of ruby reds and emerald greens. A tiny black feather broke free and swirled in coiled circles; Camille's discarded gris-gris.

Clyde's tear-soaked face bent closer to Mandy, still safe in his arms. He said, "She's gone. Our Hannah's gone."

AUTHOR'S NOTES

"Relay the Force Pattern as a Source of Tension…"

This sentence is literally an explanation of how reality is created, based on beliefs and intense emotions with intent toward action. In other words, intent on creating form, which is what happens in this physical world we live in. The planet Earth. Contrary to popular understanding, we don't believe something when we see it, we see something when we believe it.

This is a giant leap. Our consciousness is not contained in the bag of skin, bones and organs we call our body. No. We are multidimensional beings.

Hannah became aware of her powers as a Voodoo priestess. Due to a lack of proper training, she launched an immoral campaign to eliminate those people who'd hurt her and those she loved. She could accomplish this from afar; remote viewing. Power such as she inherited must be tempered with knowledge and experience and the maturity gained through tutelage under the existing High Priestess.

Clyde understood the protocol involved. He was aware of all this. His grandfather had taught him the ways of Voodooism from the time he turned three years old. Prior to that age, the mind-consciousness hasn't developed enough to form its own beliefs. In this early stage, the infant is a sponge, a ready receptacle for those around him. The newly birthed human will inculcate the beliefs of the adults who care for them. The adults hold much power for children at these young ages.

When puberty arrives, these same youngsters begin to discard some beliefs in exchange for their own.

Hannah's early years were disrupted with her being trapped in circumstances beyond her control with lascivious men who subjected her to their vulgar sexual fantasies and sadistic proclivities. This anger at the abuse she suffered made it agreeable to use her formidable powers to exact revenge, including murder.

Mandy Rose and Sophie will need to understand Hannah's role in African-based, spiritual Louisiana Voodoo. Hannah will evolve into a magnificent High Priestess; known and revered by many in the Voodoo religion.

Louisiana Voodoo, also known as New Orleans Voodoo, is an African Diasporic religion originating in Louisiana, now in the southern United States. It arose through a process of syncretism between the traditional religions of West Africa, the Roman Catholic form of Christianity and Haitian Vodou.

Louisiana Voodoo altars are constructed by many who practice Voodoo. Clyde Boudreaux's mix of Catholic statues, Voodoo dolls and religious artifacts in the small room in his house is a perfect example of one such altar.

The last scene in "The Curse of Hannah" gives us a peek into a less-familiar system of reality than most people are accustomed to being aware of.

There are untold millions of other physical realities and nonphysical realities. There is not just one dimension of consciousness, any more than there is just one country on your planet, or one planet in your solar system.

Back to "Relay the Force Pattern as a Source of Tension…" This sentence appeared to me, CJ Knapp, in the dream state, in giant red block letters.

Understand this… No reality exists that has not been created by Consciousness.

On our planet Earth, which is by our own self-proclaimed laws; a physical reality, a creation formed from Consciousness. Some other realities use Consciousness to create less permanent structures. An easy-to-understand example is your dream state. Creation but without physical form.

Look in your mirror and view how your Conscious beliefs, thoughts and intents have created your world.

So, patterns emerge and when a stage of entropy is reached; meaning that "pattern has plateaued because it's reached a stage of fullness, then it must somehow change; it will either disintegrate and a new existing reality occurs or it will dissolve into spent matter as with Clyde's house.

Hannah moved to a new plateau to achieve the magnificent role of High Priestess. She will take the place of her new guardian and teacher, Mambo; who will have served her time and will joyfully move on to a nonphysical reality; known by mortals, through a passage, called "death."

Death is not traumatic as it is commonly perceived. It's a freeing of soul. A releasing out of the cage of the human body.

Being born is much more of a shocking event. First entry into physical existence feels disturbing and fraught with fear, even though it's chosen by the new essence. Most infants bawl at the prospect of being held in a physical shell without the accustomed freedoms inherent in non-physical dimensions. The soul/entity is shocked at being newly ensconced in a body that feels solid. The more accurate truth is that nothing is solid or permanent. We purposely forget our multidimensional selves for the purity of the Earth experience. We take the curriculum. We are convinced that our challenges and problems are thrust upon us, forgetting that we are captains of our own ships, manufacturers of our own dramas.

Delightfully, young children are still quite connected to the nonphysical worlds and display charming and endearing behaviors. This includes so-called "imaginary playmates." They also often retain some of their psychic abilities and are able to "know" when a family member or friend is about to "translate"—die.

Some people maintain a more intense relationship with the larger truths of who and what we are. These folks may even have an ongoing relationship with inner beings or other aspects of their own entity, often appearing to be mentally ill to nonunderstanding onlookers. This may often include medical professionals.

I hope you've enjoyed the Hannah Series: *Who Took Hannah*, *The Search for Hannah* and this novel, *The Curse of Hannah*.

Please consider my nonfiction offering *The Secrets of Skinny;* twenty diets explained. See how many you have "tried." The little book with big answers; physical and metaphysical. A unique look at the problems of obesity.

I write under the pen name CJ Knapp.

Thank you for reading this far.

I remain ever appreciative of your time and attention.

You are wondrous beings, capable of miracles. Do not doubt yourselves.

Carole Knapp Johnson

Please consider leaving a review on social media and where you purchased the books. Your honest opinion is appreciated.

Thank you.

CJ Knapp – author